Bell

Park

Reneé Porter

Roet Press   Plantation, FL

DEDICATION

For Elizabeth, who makes her own future with her indomitable and fearless spirit.

ACKNOWLEDGMENTS

This book would not exist without those who have maintained the history of Huntington through their meticulous and incredible record keeping, photographs, and films. For early information on Cabell County and the establishment of Huntington, I must cite a rare copy I was given of George Selden Wallace's *Cabell County Annals and Families.*

I must also note the marvelous Special Collections section of the Marshall University Library System. Marshall's wonderful collection of photographs of the 1937 flood alone were invaluable in my research, as well as their history of the humble Marshall Academy that became Marshall University.

I also must note the memories of that period by citizens of Huntington such as Bob Mott, who very kindly never failed to answer the dozens of questions I asked of him, including his memories of the flood, the city streets, railroads, and people from that time. His information and anecdotes were priceless coming from someone who lived through the devastating flood.

I must acknowledge those women who gave up so much and who still inspired this story. While Julia Chafin Bell is a fictional woman, she is also an amalgam of the women in my life who came before me, from my great-grandmother, Jane Chafin, the first of five generations of my family who attended Marshall, to my grandmother Bess, whose story of the typhus epidemic was based on her on experience and loss. Her heartbreak has been the most difficult thing I have ever written.

I must once more thank the friends and family who are becoming accustomed to my obsession with writing and simply trying to tell a good story. To them, especially Rob, I can never completely express my love and gratitude.

And finally, a thanks to my editor, P. J., at Roet Press, who always encourages my daily grind.

To those of you who are unfamiliar with Huntington, I hope that as you who read *Bell Park*, you will come to love Huntington and Marshall as much as I do.

Reneé Porter

Chapter One

Summer 2010

Juls woke that morning feeling tired from running from Komodo Dragons in her dream. In the dream, the dragons ran round her as if herding her closer and closer to the sea.

As she showered for work she thought of the dragons as the hot water poured against her. The shower still had the pale aqua tiles her mother had "updated" it with in 1972 and with a small frosted window that allowed the morning sunlight to flow into the bathroom and bathe her in a natural light.

She lived in the house her grandfather had first owned in the early 1940s. It was an adaptation of a California bungalow, a small house tucked onto the hillside of what had begun as an early 20th century housing development in her hometown. Her grandparents and parents had lived there and now she lived there alone.

When she closed her eyes as she washed her hair, she could see the dragons circling her while meaningless words from an unrecognizable language were repeated in her brain like some tuneless chant. The dream had been so vivid that she could visualize the texture of their hides and their long and somewhat slimy split tongues. She thought of the words bouncing around inside her head and tried to connect the dragons and the sounds as if she were solving one of the logic problems she often worked as a method to drive away her nightly insomnia, but none of it made much sense.

Maybe the dream was a left over last night from watching Paul Bettany as Charles Darwin in *Creation* on Netflix. The movie had certainly been depressing enough to have seeded itself into some wee part of her brain because she knew that the Komodo Dragons were found in Indonesia, not in the Galapagos.

She sighed and began to put on her make-up. She dressed, gathered her papers for work, grabbed her keys and spent a long and quiet morning thinking of the dragons driving her across the sand to the seawater. She thought maybe the language was some South Pacific island language, but she had never had any desire to visit the South Pacific. She felt as if her head were trying to tell her something, but her brain might as well have been addressing her in Mandarin for all the sense it made.

She did live a quiet life, but it was of her own choice. She spent her days in a turn of the century house downtown in what was probably once someone's beautiful second storey bedroom, her desk situated before a large bay window that faced the southwest.

Each day was a simple routine of editing press releases and advertising copy for Turner and Schulte, a small public relations firm which specialized in financial institutions as clients. She never met the clients. She never visited the firms. She did not even know what the buildings of her clients looked like or even what the clients looked like and she wrote for them without really caring. She had a good job – not an easy thing to find with a liberal arts English degree. She often thought that her luck might have been better had she chosen an English education degree, but the two paths gave her a choice between a class in learning to use audio visual equipment or learning a foreign language. She chose French and left the path to teaching.

C'est la vie, she often mused, wondering if she might have been a good teacher. Her father certainly had been. He had been loved by his geology students at Marshall and he found the field trips exhilarating. During her childhood years, her home had been filled with young students bringing specimens and talking with her dad as her mother worked in the kitchen fixing meals and snacks for all of them.

It was a happy childhood and Juls liked the students, but she didn't think she could inspire anyone to such a passionate love of their work, Perhaps, she sometimes thought, because she held little passion for her own work.

She had started out with the company as a copywriter six years ago, shortly after graduating from Marshall University. By her fifth year there, she was the company's editorial director and answered only to the owner of the company, John Schulte, who always spoke with the clients. His partner, Ed Turner, had left two decades earlier, but Schulte liked the idea of potential clients thinking of his company as a partnership so he kept Turner's name on the door even though Turner had left town when he left Schulte behind.

It was an easy job, one that never tasked her and that held a routine that was both comfortable and expected.

Her evenings were spent either alone or with a few close friends who never really knew much about her other than the brief history she had given them. She did not purposefully hide anything from them and she did not lie. She simply failed to give them any more information that she felt they needed. She sometimes went out with them to Max & Erma's restaurant or a movie at Pullman Square. Sometimes she went to a Marshall Artist Series event at the Keith Albee Theatre with a date. But she often came home alone. Again, a choice of her own.

But the truth of whom she really was would have surprised her friends and colleagues.

She was Julia Louisa Bell, known to all as "Juls", and she lived in Bell Park in Huntington, West Virginia. To most people, including her neighbors in Bell Park, that meant nothing. She was their neighbor – a young woman who lived in another Craftsman style house perched on a very large lot at the back of the Park. The house had been given to her by her parents when they had left Huntington for Boca Raton about the same time she had gone to work for Turner & Schulte. Most of the people who knew her parents knew as little about them as they did about her. Sometimes someone would comment on her surname and the name of where she lived, but they usually did so in jest, never knowing if there was a connection between the two.

She could have probably spent her entire life without anyone knowing anything important about her had the man not knocked on her door the evening after she had dreamed of the dragons. She answered it without looking outside first, thinking that it was possibly a neighbor with some question or request. Bell Park was secluded from the main part of Huntington and few people who did not live there ever found a reason to go there since it was not really a park, just a name of an isolated section of the city.

So when Juls opened the door and found the man at her door holding what appeared to be a tablet computer within his folded arms, she suddenly remembered the dragons and frowned.

She did not like surprises or strangers. She liked her orderly routine with a small roster of people she allowed to have access to her life.

Her frown must have given him a different impression of her and he stepped back from the door. He really wasn't an unusual man. He was on the whole a normal looking man, perhaps 35 or 40, with brown hair that was starting to recede a bit. He was neither tall nor short, normal weight, and eyes that actually were hidden by heavy tortoise shell frames. His most distinguishing feature might have been his very broad shoulders buried under a white oxford cloth shirt and navy blue sports coat. He certainly had no rough hide and as far as she could tell, no split tongue. And that thought made her suddenly smile.

He pushed his glasses up and held out one hand to introduce himself.

"I hope I'm not bothering you. I'm looking for, uh," he paused and consulted the tablet, "for Julia Bell."

He looked up to find the woman at the door unresponsive.

"My name is Jack Robbins. I'm writing a history of the Collis Huntington railroad empire and I came here from New York to research Huntington as the western terminus of the line. I thought I'd try to speak to Ms. Bell, but everyone said I should come here, so if you're not Ms. Bell, would you know where I could find her?"

He stopped and again waited for her response, but none came.

"I apologize for appearing so abruptly and I would have called, but her number was unlisted and . . ." he said, unsure as to how to continue what was increasingly becoming a one sided conversation.

The minute he had said Collis Huntington and railroad she had frowned again. Until that point, she had had a brief moment of curiosity about the man, but she lost all interest then. She knew exactly why he was here and she had no desire whatsoever to talk with him about what he wanted to discuss.

"I'm sorry," she said interrupting his small speech. "I am Julia Bell, but I'm going out and really can't talk with you. If you're interested in early Huntington history, you might try the local history room at either the downtown library or the special collections over at Marshall University. I'm sure you'll find more information on Huntington at either place," and she began to close the door in the man's face.

But he reached his hand out to her again and looked pleadingly at her, "I've already gotten everything I can from those sources. I need to talk to someone whose family was involved with the railroad. I was hoping that the Bell family might have something that the libraries didn't have, since they were so involved with the railroad," he paused and then added "Please, any help would be invaluable."

She sighed inwardly. He wasn't going to go away, but she wasn't going to allow him to enter her home, either.

"I really have plans this evening, but I could meet with you tomorrow around noon at Marshall."

He smiled brightly. "That would be great. Where on campus would be good?"

She bit her lip for a moment trying to think of a place that was public, yet would afford her some privacy if the discussion took the direction she expected it to take.

"The library. Second floor. But, please be as punctual as possible. I only have a short time to talk with you," she replied.

"I really appreciate your taking the time to talk with me.," he said reaching his hand out again.

Damn, she thought. He was one very determined man about trying to shake hands. She reluctantly took his hand

and was surprised to find his handshake firm and strong and his skin just a bit rough.

"And call me Juls. No one calls me Julia," she said as she shook his hand.

As he began to walk away from her house, he was stopped by her voice from the porch. He turned back towards her and could barely make out her form on the porch in the falling twilight.

She knew she should have left at that point and should have planned to stand him up tomorrow, but something about him made her stop him and ask the question to which she already knew the answer.

"Are you really here to ask about Jonas Bell and the murder?"

The man stopped and looked around the neighborhood. Lights were beginning to appear in the windows of some houses and he could hear in the distance the voices of children being called in for the evening. He knew that she was not going to like his response, but he told her the truth nonetheless.

"Yes. I am."

Ok, he thought, here's where she disappears.

When he again heard no response from her, he saw that as a bad sign. She could hold the key to the mystery of what had really happened to Jonas Bell. He squinted to see if she were still standing on the porch. He could barely see her white shirt now.

"I see," she said rather too quietly. "I will see you tomorrow," and she turned and reentered her home without any other reaction or words.

He walked away from the house and got into his Honda rental. Before leaving, he took one last look at the bungalow and still saw no light or movements from within it. As he drove away, he thought of Jonas Bell and what the man's dreams had become. It all seemed a bit sad after meeting her.

But inside the foyer, Juls Bell leaned back against the shut door and closed her eyes tightly. The dragons had arrived and she could swim away or face them, but they had arrived with the man with the tablet and she feared her quiet life was not likely to ever be quiet again.

Chapter Two

Summer 2010

Jack Robbins arrived 45 minutes earlier than Juls had asked of him. He wanted to take no chances of missing her. He knew he might not get a second chance at talking with her and at this point, she might be his last hope. He sat at a table near a bright window and had his tablet out, a legal pad, and some photocopies he had made of news stories about Juls's great-grandfather, Jonas.

He leaned back in the hard plastic chair and watched the sidewalk below that led to the entrance of the library. The spring semester was winding down to finals week and students seemed to be preoccupied, probably with finals and summer plans.

A part of him did not expect Juls Bell to meet him, but she was the only one who might have the answers he needed and so he waited rather despondently.

His book had originally been a history on the Huntington Railroad, but he had been losing interest quickly in Collis Huntington until the discovery of the Jonas Bell scandal had taken him in a different direction. The more he learned about Jonas, the more he was taken in by the man who had died over 60 years ago. He wondered if Jonas had had that effect on people during his lifetime.

Either way, Jonas had changed Jack's book and truthfully had taken over his life. Jonas, well, Jonas was a man who had had everything and had died with nothing but a resentful family and a horrible reputation.

It was fifteen minutes past noon and he was beginning to stack his papers to put back in his briefcase when Juls appeared at the other end of the table. He looked up over the top of his glasses and at first thought he was imagining the tall, young woman standing there in a well tailored blue pinstripe suit, a frown still creasing what appeared to be otherwise very pleasant and refined features.

She made him feel unkempt and somewhat schlumpy. He wasn't wearing a jacket today and for some idiotic reason he felt as if he had ink smeared on his face, which he stupidly tried to rub away as if it were really there.

Everything about her was so very neatly packaged, from her smooth manicured hands to her clean and shining ash blonde hair pulled back with a baroque gold and pearl hair clip. She carried nothing with her. No purse. No briefcase. Nothing. She sat down next to him at the table and placed her hands flat on the table and looked to him as if expecting him to begin his questions without even an acknowledgement of her arrival.

And, so he did. He put the tablet in his briefcase and left only the legal pad and pen in front of him to make notes if he needed.

He began with the most obvious question, but one that had to be asked first nevertheless.

"Was Jonas Bell your great-grandfather?"

"Yes," she said without emotion.

He bit his lower lip for a moment and nodded. He might as well ask the big question now. If she were going to run or refuse his questions, she would at least have to respond in some way to the most important question he had.

"Did he or perhaps I should ask, do you think, he killed his mother? Your great-great grandmother . . . um, Julia? I didn't notice till now that you shared her name."

Her nostrils flared slightly, but no other hint of emotion crossed her face. She looked into his eyes before answering. In the brighter light of the library, he appeared to be a handsomer man than she had initially thought and she saw something, but she wasn't sure what, in his eyes behind those awful dark glasses.

"First, tell me what you think you know," she replied.

He had picked up his pen, preparing to write, but now laid it back down, folding his arms in front of himself on the table and leaning toward her.

"Ok. According to what I've found in different source records, Jonas Bell was the son of one the men who served as a liaison of Collis Huntington here in Huntington. Bell was thought to have come into some financial difficulties in the 1930s and was thought by some to even have a gambling problem," Jack said.

"Lots of speculation on him. I even found an article about his, uh, situation in the New York Times archives."

He pulled his notes out again and looked through them to see if he had missed anything in his short speech.

Jack ceased his recitation of his notes for a moment to see if Juls were reacting in any way. Still, he saw no emotions there. She was very self-controlled, he thought.

"Jonas's mother was murdered in 1937 and he was the number one suspect. She was found in her parlor by her housemaid. She had been stabbed in the neck and," he paused and decided not to mention that in some accounts he had read that the woman had nearly been decapitated.

"Her jewelry was missing as well as her money and some things from her upstairs safe. The local police believed Jonas had committed the murder, but they were never able to prove anything. The jewelry and bonds were never found. A local charity inherited her estate, but no money was included and if there was money, it was never found at the time he died."

Juls pursed her lips and then smiled. "That's been the big question my family has been asking since Jonas died."

"As to your original question," she continued, "I don't know. Of course, I never knew him. He died years before I was born and my father never spoke much about him. I know many of the same things you've just said - that his father worked for Collis Huntington and my family was once wealthy. I know that Jonas's mother was murdered. I know that he was the chief suspect. I know that he was indicted or arrested for the murder, but was released before trial. Beyond that I know very little."

Jack sighed. He already knew everything she had just said. He had hoped for some information that the family had withheld. He had nothing to continue with if this were all the information she had to offer.

"I'm sorry," she said. "It's never been a story of which my family has been particularly proud. Jonas may well have killed her. The disappearance of the family money was a horrible blow for those he left behind. My father was a geology professor at Marshall who attended school on scholarships. My grandfather sold real estate for someone else in the very place Jonas had started – Bell Park. No one knows what Jonas did with any of the money. Even if he did murder his mother, nothing was ever found. Nothing. It was pathetic, I suppose, for a family who had been one of the early families of Huntington to end up penniless with Jonas's crime painting everything in their lives."

Jack listened carefully, hoping that something, anything, might come out of this conversation. He actually felt a small pang of pity for Juls. She hadn't done anything wrong. She had simply been born a Bell. He wondered for the first time if many people really knew her family history.

"I didn't mean to be rude to you yesterday. I do not like to discuss what happened with Jonas or my great-great grandmother." She glanced around the room, watching students with backpacks passing by, each of them absorbed in his or her own little world. While it had only been six years ago that she had been one of them, it now felt as if it had been a lifetime ago. She wondered why for the first time she had not allowed herself to dream about a life away from this place and the curse that seemed to hang over her family.

"I don't talk about it with anyone. You may be the first person I've ever told about Jonas. Not even the local media have ever contacted me about him. I've always preferred it that way."

Jack was beginning to feel like a bit of a jerk now. She really didn't know much of the story at all. The people involved in the story may have been family members, but they had as much to do with her as he did with his own ancestors.

He looked at her face. He realized that during her entire recitation of her knowledge of the murder that she had not looked at him one time.

"What about your dad? Do you think he might know something?"

Juls shook her head. "Dad rarely talks about his grandfather. He had a tough time of it growing up. The family had no money, but enough people were still left alive who remembered the scandal. It was hard on him. Very hard on him."

"And before you ask me, no, I won't ask him. He's been through enough with that part of his family. Damn. The only reason it hasn't come back at me is that almost everyone who was involved is dead or has forgotten it or they don't know who I am," she continued, this time her voice becoming terse with anger.

Jack stopped for a moment and removed his glasses, rubbed his eyes and then looked at her.

"I'm sorry for showing up and presuming you had all the answers I was looking for. I just was at a point in the book where everything seemed to come to a dead stop, well, poor choice of words."

"Can you remember anything that might help? A conversation you might have overheard as a child or photographs or any family papers?" he asked.

She smiled a little. She knew he had more questions and that he would continue asking questions. She saw that she could not get rid of him with just this short meeting.

"Why should I share any of this with you? How can I know that you won't paint my entire family as if they were the Borgias with no attempt at truth?"

She was absolutely right, he thought. Why should she trust him? He had known some writers who would have simply created links where none existed. He had no idea how to convince her that he would not.

She looked him in the eyes and knew that he would write this with or without her help. Perhaps if she did help, she could convince him to at least be fair.

The dragons had come back in her dreams again this morning. She had expected this, had known it on some subconscious level. She laughed quietly and began to think that she might understand Mandarin more than she had thought.

"Alright. Today is Thursday. I will give you this weekend. Meet me at my house around six tomorrow. We can begin then," she said and stood and started to walk away.

"What changed your mind?" Jack asked.

"Dragons," she said and laughed as she walked away.

Jack leaned back in the chair once more. She was not one for either saying hello or goodbye, he thought, and she was one of the most unusual women he had ever met. There were many aspects to her that he knew he was not seeing.

Why had she changed her mind? He shook his head and finished putting his things together. He wondered if she would be more receptive tomorrow or simply deceptive. Either way, he was going to try.

Chapter Three

January 12, 1937

Julia Chafin Bell sat in her solarium watching the coal barges on the Ohio make their way inevitably toward the Mississippi. Every afternoon she took tea in the solarium, surrounded by the palms and exotic orchids she had collected through the years. She could sit there among them undisturbed by the city that had grown up around her home, now just one of the many riverside homes spread along the Ohio down to the Sixth Street bridge in the center of downtown Huntington.

She would be 78 in May and she had lived here and known the land here long before Collis Huntington and his railroad had brought his "progress" and money to her father's farm land. Oh, she knew that her father had been well remunerated for the purchase and that she had become the prize to be won by Mr. Huntington's lackeys, but she missed the time before the city had existed, before she had had to become a lady, when she was still a young girl with the illusion of a freedom to choose her own destiny.

How naïve we are when we're young, she thought. She had actually thought that McKenzie Bell had wanted her above everything else. He had not been the man she had thought she was marrying and he not been a good husband. He simply was the father of her children, the man who used her great dowry to build this ridiculous mansion, and the man who spent more time with the whores on Second Avenue than he did with her. At least he had had the good grace to die before he had spent all her money, of which she had no doubt he would have done.

In 1904, at 45, she had been left a widow who had borne her husband two sons and one daughter. Her oldest son had died of typhus after the 1891 flood and she had almost succumbed to the disease herself. She had been so delirious with grief and the fever that she had hidden under a bed, afraid that McKenzie would find her and kill her.

She watched as two more barges passed on the river and sipped her tea in the precious Wedgewood china cups that were part of the window dressing she had been required by McKenzie in order to maintain herself as an "elite" citizen of the city and which she had unfortunately been left to continue as a "Grande Dame" of Huntington society. She always found that designation as hypocritical as the attention paid to her opinion by certain women in the city. If new residents only knew that she would always be the daughter of a farmer, a girl who grew up in a large farmhouse, often running wild with her brothers along the banks of the great muddy river, they might have thought differently of her.

"Grande Dames" were never the daughters of farmers, yet some of the women who became "old" Huntington society were exactly that – the daughters of farmers who had sold their large farms to Collis Huntington and who had used that new found wealth to mimic the east coast society that Huntington represented to them.

But McKenzie had taught her the lesson of being a prosperous and mannered wife shortly after they were married by forbidding her to leave their home without an escort and without informing him first of where she would be. She learned that calls were never made without leaving a calling card the day before. She also was taught the protocol of whom she should see and whom she should shun. And high tea, God how she had come to hate that, and yet here she was, having it over 60 years later, alone. She remembered sitting with women she had once known as children running the fields of their family farms with her who later pretended that all that had come before Huntington's railroad had never happened, that they had always been well born, well tutored women.

All visits and visitors had to be approved by McKenzie first. At the age of 17 she had gone from being a river spirit to a groomed and gilded prisoner whose duties included church, charity, and planning the new city's social events.

She despised the name placed on her family's land. Guyandotte was not the name of the planned city envisioned by Mr. Huntington or McKenzie and his compatriots. No, Mr. Huntington had to have his own name there. Fat bastard.

She smiled to herself at that. Her brother Christopher had called him that when he realized that Huntington had taken his future away from him when he was forced to leave West Virginia and work for the Huntington railroad.

No, "Fat Bastard" was not a name that a "Grande Dame" would use. But, deep inside her, the river child still existed, even 63 years later. She allowed herself a small smile at that thought.

Now, with her family spread across the country, she only had her two children still living here in Huntington and she rarely saw either of them, although Jonas, her son, lived in a smaller mansion just a few acres from her own home. He lived there with his wife Louisa and their son Mack, though Mack had just returned from West Virginia University and would probably be starting his own family sometime in the next few years.

Julia's only remaining daughter, Thea, named after Julia's late mother, was married to a man who had lost most of his money during the depression. Thea and her children were completely dependent on an allowance granted them by Julia with a strict stipulation that the money be administered by Julia's lawyer. Thea's husband, angered by Julia's terms, left to work somewhere in Texas and never again contacted his wife or children. He sent them no money. They were completely dependent on Julia's largesse.

Julia felt regret for Thea's situation, but she had had to be practical or Thea's husband would have wasted the money on one scheme after another. Julia had known he was a lazy man from the first time she had met him, but what could she do? Thea was not a very handsome woman and not very intelligent and she could be petty and mean. She would be past a marriageable age if Julia had not allowed her marriage to Reginald Harris, but Julia had spent many sleepless nights worrying over the grief that Harris the wastrel would bring her daughter.

At least I eventually saw McKenzie for what he was shortly after our marriage, she thought, rather than maintaining some sick self-deception that he might turn into a decent man. Poor Thea had never seen the truth about her spouse.

Had the good lord not seen fit to take McKenzie when he did, she herself might have been just as miserable. Julia thought that perhaps her greatest strength had been her ability to discern a person's true personality. She was greatly saddened that she had not possessed that ability at 17 or that Thea had never shared that trait.

Thea had bought a home a few blocks from the park that had been donated to the city by the Ritter family. She was raising her family there. She held to the pretense for all Huntington society to see that her husband was so seriously involved in the railroad business that he could rarely find time to visit Huntington.

But Huntington society was not blind and were it not for her mother's position, Thea would have become a pitied idiot, ripe for their derision.

Julia sat in her solarium and suddenly felt very old. She was so tired of the role McKenzie and Huntington had placed upon her. She thought of the river child she had been, running through the reeds near the ferry landing, the warm summer wind always blowing across the Ohio, tangling her hair as she chased Christopher. She used to lie on the bank in the tall green and golden grass and watch the clouds passing overhead, not knowing that one day soon that that freedom would be stolen from her.

She had chosen McKenzie with her father's urging and because he was a handsome and dapper young man. She had imagined that she was in love with him and he, of course, had known just the right words with which to woo her.

They had married in June 1876, shortly after her 17th birthday and had taken the train to Chicago for their honeymoon. She had prepared that first night on the train for him. By the time he returned to their sleeping car, he passed out asleep with the smell of bourbon pouring from his gaping mouth, interspersed with loud drunken snores emanating from him. Not the knight in shining armor she had envisioned with his recitation of poetry to her before the wedding.

So, she waited for the second night and he had come to her to consummate their marriage. But, he was drunk again and unfortunately this time, instead of passing out, he had ripped her nightclothes from her and savagely pushed himself into her without any tenderness or love. It was a painful, humiliating rape of her innocence both physically and emotionally and sadly the shape of their future lovemaking.

Oh, she had fought him off as she as become older, calling him an oaf and telling him to go to one of his women on Second Avenue, but every so often, whether she chose it or not, he had his way and she lay there each time with tears streaming down her face. Were it not for the children that she bore so easily, she would have thrown herself into the river long ago. Only for them did she survive him and by the time he was gone she had become frozen into the role proscribed for her by Huntington itself.

Sometimes when she was driven around town by her driver Curtis, she would see the young female coeds emerging from the Morrow Library at Marshall College . She was filled with great sadness for Anne Morrow Lindbergh whose father Dwight had helped fund the James E. Morrow Library in 1930. Anne Lindbergh's grandfather, James, had been principal of Marshall College for several years. Julia could not pass that library without thinking of the tragedy that had befallen young Anne and she often wondered if all women were born to suffer pain as she had been taught in church while growing up.

As Julia watched the coeds come and go, she felt both jealousy for their freedom and sadness for her cage. She was too old to escape her cage now, but she could wield her money and power and sometimes, without anyone's knowledge except for her lawyer, she would sponsor one of those young women with the condition that they use their education to help other women escape the traps of spousal servitude and poverty.

It made her feel as if part of herself escaped with some of those young women and while nothing could take from her the wrongs that had been committed against her, she was happy that in some small way she had helped a few of them avoid the cage she had allowed herself to be placed within.

Julia Chafin Bell sat and watched the men on the coal barges and sipped her tea. She would have wept had she been a weaker woman.

Chapter Four

Summer 2010

The great-great granddaughter of Julia Chafin Bell had become everything that her ancestor would have wanted. She had her own home, a good job, her own money, and she answered to no man. But she was alone and her ancestor would have recognized something that even her namesake could not see – that being free was not always enough to bring happiness.

So her namesake was trying to understand why she was considering going into her family's attic to look for any photograph albums or journals or records of what her family had been for a man she did not know, a man who could very well ruin her life by dredging up the sad and pathetic history of the Bell family.

She could hear her father now.

"Juls, what the hell are you doing? Let it go. Leave it in the past. Go on with your life and forget the rest of it."

But for some reason. she could not. She thought perhaps that she wanted to know the truth as well. Am I the descendant of a murderer, she asked herself, although part of herself truly didn't care. She was who she was, not a woman marked by Jonas or the Bell name. But still, the question hung in her subconscious, just as the dragons hunted her in her morning dreams.

There were boxes in the small attic that held mostly papers from her grandfather's family and her parents' history. She had moved boxes from one side of the attic to the other and had found nothing when she saw a small latch on the wall next to the back stairwell. She lifted it, finding it revealed an almost indiscernible door along the bead board paneling of the attic wall. She opened the small door which was a bit jammed by time and the summer humidity of swollen wood. Even the light in the attic was not strong enough to illuminate the space. She went down to the kitchen and returned with a flashlight and at first saw nothing there, but as she aimed the light toward the back of the space, she spied an old humpback trunk shoved all the way to the far wall.

Somehow she squeezed her tall frame partially into the space and found she could only reach the trunk with one hand and that hand was not nearly strong enough to pull the weight of the trunk to her.

Just as she was beginning to get angry, she heard the doorbell and realized that Jack Robbins was at her door. She backed herself out of the space, brushed the dirt off her clothes and headed downstairs to open the door for him.

When she opened the door his smile turned into a look of puzzlement. She nevertheless smiled and asked him to enter her home, then excused herself for a moment to wash her hands off.

It was only when she looked into the bathroom mirror that she realized why he had appeared so puzzled. Her face was filthy and her blonde hair was covered in cobwebs.

Oh, Jesus, she thought. Just what I need.

While she was washing her face and combing the cobwebs from her hair, Jack sat in her living room and looked around at the antique Stickley furniture she had scavenged through the years to furnish the house with. He was stunned by the money she had in the Arts and Crafts furniture that dominated the room. Just the armchairs alone would have cost him an advance on his next book. And they all looked in pristine condition with the original leather cushions and hand wrought hardware. He was standing next to one of the two bookcases on each side of the fireplace, looking at her collection of first editions from the first half of the 20th century when she returned.

"You have an amazing house," he said to her as she entered the room.

She smiled and said "Thank you" without further elaboration on how she had come to own such an incredible collection of furniture or books.

He wasn't going to let her get away with her monosyllabic answers tonight.

"Did you do this or were these family things?"

"They're mine. I thought the furniture was best suited for the house and the book collection began much earlier, even before I decided to major in English," she replied.

He sat down in one of the armchairs. "You majored in English? Do you teach?"

She laughed. "No, I write for a public relations firm here in town. Well, at least I used to write. Now I just edit everyone else's work. Fairly boring stuff."

"I thought you knew this," she said, "what with all the research you've been doing."

He shook his head. "No, I was more or less focused on Jonas and his era. As I mentioned in the library, I only found that you existed by accident when I was following a family genealogy at the downtown library."

"Oh, yes," she said. "Thea's tome. She did quite a job of whitewashing the family name, didn't she?"

Jack smiled at her. She had a very dry sense of humor that he was only beginning to comprehend. She wasn't cold, but she was still a bit defensive. Cold was a tough façade to break, but defensiveness was just a little easier if the right tact was used.

"May I ask why you had cobwebs in your hair when I arrived?" he asked.

Juls had known he would eventually ask about it. She made the decision when she answered the door to enlist his help in removing the trunk from its hiding place. If there were things there that the family had hidden, so be it. Without his help, she knew she couldn't get the trunk out.

"Actually, I found something in the attic, but I can't manage it by myself. Want to help?"

Jack was on his feet faster than she expected and she stood slowly, still wary of sharing a potential treasure of information with him. Of course, the trunk could also hold nothing but old 1950s real estate brochures or shredded and mouldering clothing from her great-great grandmother's generation. Removing it from the crawlspace might be a completely useless endeavor.

"It's upstairs. Follow me," she said leading him through the dining room to the tiny stairwell that led to the attic.

"It's an old trunk. I only found it when I was moving boxes around up there. I hope you don't have dust allergies. I think I might have destroyed a civilization of dust mites trying to get to the damned thing."

Jack laughed. "No, no dust allergies, though I have to admit to an intense dislike of mold."

At the top of the steps, Juls pointed out the small door and explained that the trunk had been pushed as far back in the small compartment as possible. Jack knelt before the door using the flashlight Juls gave him so he could see the trunk. Whoever had placed it there had not intended it to be accessible to anyone, that much he could ascertain. He also knew that he could not possibly reach it. His shoulders alone would prevent his accessing the compartment, though his arms might be long enough to grasp the leather handle he could see on the side.

"Well, I don't think I can get to it either, which leaves us two choices. We can cut through the wall," he said.

"Absolutely not," Juls said.

"Or, as I was about to say, we could attach a rope or chain to it, using a hook or even a bent wire coat hanger, well at least you could, and then I could pull it closer to the door," he continued.

"Sorry. Yes, I have a chain in the garden shed out back and there are some old wire hangers in one of those boxes," she said. "I'll go get the chain while you work on forming a hook from one of the hangers."

Once again he was left alone in part of her home and again he felt strangely uncomfortable in the house.

He sighed and thought, well I am an intruder. While he found himself attracted to Juls, he did not feel any connection to her or her home beyond the mystery of the murder that seemed to be driving him since he had first read of it. Maybe it was guilt, he thought. Maybe not. Either way, finding a wire hanger was his current task and that was not going to be as easy as Juls had seemed to think it was.

Two things hindered his search – first, the attic was full of old boxes. They were piled all around him, even covering some old pieces of furniture and blocking the furniture in some places. The second problem was the light. What little natural light that had been in the attic from the lone front window was fading to darkness, leaving him with the dim light from the downstairs door and the small beam from the flashlight. He eventually located a wire hanger in one of the boxes and had just begun untwisting one as Juls returned with a six foot length of lightweight brass chain.

Jack took the chain and fastened one end of the twisted and now double-hooked wire hanger to it and handed the hook to Juls.

"See if you can squeeze through the door enough to try and hook the handle of the trunk with the hanger," he said.

Juls curled the upper part of her body around the entrance and tossed the hook at the handle.

"Shit," she said and then quickly apologized. "Sorry. This sounded like a good idea, but it's hard."

She uncurled herself and sat up wiping the sweat from her forehead, leaving a dark trail of dirt across it. Jack laughed.

"Now, I'm sorry. Want to stop?" he asked.

"Good god, no. Now I want that trunk out of there more than ever," she said and curled back again around the door facing. It took three tries before she finally managed to get the hook securely attached to the leather handle.

"Ok. It's hooked."

She joined Jack outside the small door and the two of them began to gently tug at the trunk. She could feel the trunk moving inches along. It was unimaginably heavy. By the time they had pulled the trunk to the opening, Jack moved in front of Juls and grabbed the leather handle to maneuver the trunk through the opening in the wall.

The light in the attic was gone now and opening the trunk there would be futile, especially if there were papers to be read. They needed the light from the downstairs floor.

"I suggest we try to get this monster into your dining room. You have better lighting there and we can get a better look at the contents," Jack said.

Juls nodded her agreement and the two of them struggled down the short flight of stairs into the dining room where for the first time they were able to get a truly good look at the trunk.

"This trunk predates this house. It's not even 20th century. The humpback shape may even date to the era when Huntington was founded," Juls said,

This time Jack nodded his agreement, though he had noticed something that Juls may not have noticed - a heavy padlock that was not as old as the trunk.

"What the hell was it doing in a crawlspace in the attic of a 1940s faux Craftsman house?" she asked.

She turned to Jack.

"You know, I'm not sure my parents even know it was up there. A lot of those boxes belonged to my grandfather, who lived here before they did. He could have hidden the door with his boxes. But maybe not. I barely saw the seam of the door in the oak paneling myself. I just don't know what to think."

Jack took a deep breath and knelt in front of the trunk, moving the lock around, tugging at it, but finding it firmly closed.

"Well, we're not going to get anything done until we get this lock off of it and I am not able to pick a lock. Are you?"

She shook her head. She hadn't the slightest idea of how it could be opened.

"Do you have any old keys around? Keys that are old but might have seemed useless other than ornamental?" he asked.

She started to reply "no" and then remembered a ring of keys in an old Hoosier cabinet in the basement. Without a word, she ran downstairs and began to go through the drawers of the cabinet until she found it.

When she returned to the dining room, she handed the ring to Jack and said, "Think one of these might work?"

He looked over the different keys. They were all skeleton keys with nothing notable. Some of them had numbers on them. He checked the back of the lock and found the number 927, then looked to see if one of the keys had the same number. None of them did, but he still tried each of them in the lock nevertheless. Well, that would have been too easy, he thought.

"Shit," Juls said,

He looked up at her in surprise. The second time she had cursed in front of him tonight and while an innocuous word, it was still not a word he expected to come from this somewhat proper young woman he had just met. He wiped sweat from his brow with his sleeve and saw dark dirt stain the arm and cuff.

"Could you possible extend your deadline of my research? I don't know about you, but I'm absolutely beat," he said.

Juls sighed in frustration, but not at him, at the damned trunk in the middle of her dining room.

"Of course, you're right.," she said. "We're both exhausted."

"The trunk will still be here tomorrow. When do you want to come by??" she asked.

Jack was a bit taken aback by her abrupt change in attitude, but hid it. She had seemed as fascinated by the enigma the trunk presented as he was. Now she was coolly indifferent.

"I'll come by around 10 tomorrow morning. I can pick up a metal saw at Home Depot and we can cut the lock off if nothing else."

She smiled in agreement and became the woman with whom he had become used to working over the past few days. She showed him to the door with few words. He was out the door in just a few minutes with barely a goodbye, left standing on her front porch and watching her shut off the lights as she went back into the house.

She was so much tougher to decipher than he had ever thought. His first impressions of her were nothing like the woman he had witnessed tonight and yet by evening's end, she was that woman again, tight lipped and unsmiling with few words for him or about anything for that matter.

As he was driving away, the thought that she might be looking for a metal saw in the basement of her house did not occur to him until he was almost out of Bell Park.

Damn it, he thought. She *had* given up too easily. Why hadn't he seen that?

He pulled into an empty driveway and turned the Honda around and headed back to her house. He'd be damned if she was going to open that trunk without him there.

Chapter Five

January 22, 1937

There was little warning for the citizens of Huntington of the flood that was about to inundate the entire downtown area, including the mansions built on Third Avenue near the railroads and the river. Julia Chafin Bell had been whisked away from her home by her son Jonas, along with his wife and son, to her daughter Thea's home near Ritter Park. And while the newer railroad tracks and two viaducts that separated the south side of town from the downtown area along the river provided a barrier of some protection, the south side area was generally saved from the flood waters, although the rain soaked ground in sections of the large park became small sodden lakes.

Some ground water pushed itself into basements and root cellars of homes in parts of the south side as well, but the Ritter Park area, including the high school and businesses beyond 8th Avenue were spared. While some homes closer to the flood zone appeared to be undisturbed by the water, their foundations shifted and many would have to have extensive repairs in the years after the flood.

Thea greeted her mother effusively, doting upon her to the point that Julia felt smothered by her ministrations. Julia had complained bitterly to Jonas on the trip across town about going to Thea's home, but to no avail. And, although she knew he was right when he pointed out that it was the nearest place to stay, she did not make mention to him that she did not feel that it was the safest.

She felt slight twinges of guilt over her inexplicable feelings toward Thea and her inability to trust Thea's sons. They fawned over her as much as their mother did, but she could feel a falsity in their claims of caring. God help her, but they often frightened her in much the same way McKenzie had. There was nothing truthful or honest about them. She had even left her good jewelry at home in her bedroom safe rather than going to Thea's wearing it. Something about the boys was not right. Something, in fact, she felt was seriously wrong.

Sometimes she wondered if she placed too many expectations on them or if she simply and wrongly misplaced her feelings about McKenzie upon them. But she knew in her heart that the feelings were not misplaced. Something was not right with them.

Thea had often complained that she made a difference between her boys and Jonas's son, Mack. Julia would protest that she did not and would try to make some small gesture, usually involving money, to demonstrate that she did not favor Mack over them. But once again, in her heart and her head, she knew she did.

Thea had placed her in a large guest room at the front of the house and the young girl who kept house for Thea had unpacked Julia's small valise and trunk by the time Julia had finally managed to convince her family that she was fine and just wished to go to bed, that she was tired from the hustle and bustle of packing and leaving her home.

As she climbed the staircase, she saw the rest of her family huddled around a giant cherry wood cathedral style Wurlitzer radio, listening for the latest news on the ever rising Ohio. Julia could hear the strains of some popular song called "Me and My Shadow" that the radio station to which they had tuned seemed insistent on playing between each news brief. After hearing the song for what felt like the fiftieth time, Julia had had enough and said goodnight to them.

This was not the first time she had seen the great river rise and it might not be the last. The river rose. The river fell. It was simply a fact of life that she could neither change nor desire to understand. If it was God's will that her home be washed away, so be it. She was steadfastly pragmatic about her or any man's ability to control or tame nature, especially the river. Only a fool such as Thea would obsess over every inch it rose.

Of course, she also did not have a great deal to lose if the Ohio flooded the downtown as some families did. She had survived the stock crash of 1929 simply because she had transferred all her money from McKenzie's stocks to land and other negotiable instruments, including some gold and jewelry which she kept in her bedroom safe. No one in the family and no servant knew of the existence of the safe. She had had her brother Christopher send someone from California to install it for her.

She sighed as she sat upon the lumpy mattress that Thea obviously thought was the proper caliber for a guest. How she had managed to have a child so oblivious to something as simple as purchasing a good mattress was beyond her.

She could see the rain blowing in against the windows in great gusts and she did feel a pang of sadness for those families who would be losing everything in this flood. There were businesses downtown which had barely made it through the past decade that would suddenly find their existence snuffed out like a candle on a nightstand.

Julia decided that either tomorrow or sometime in the next few days that she would visit her lawyer Allen Perry and make arrangements for some of the better, yet small and struggling businesses to receive an anonymous donation to help them get back on solid ground.

She did not want to do this around her family and thought that if all else failed, she could have Thea's driver take her to the Perry home on some vague, but urgent, business manner.

When it came to money, they were all afraid to say anything to her. And, she knew why. She was rich and she was old and they did not want to risk being removed from her will. That thought made her laugh out loud in the quiet bedroom. She was leaving them nothing beyond what they had already received from her. That would certainly be a surprise for them.

Chapter Six

Summer 2010

When Jack rang the bell at Juls's house just a few minutes after leaving her, he had not expected to have been greeted by her so quickly. And when he saw the blood on her shirt, he became very concerned.

"What the hell . . . ?" he asked as he entered the foyer.

She was already running back toward the kitchen, drops of blood trailing behind her. He ran after her and found her at the sink trying to staunch the flow of blood from a large gash across her left palm. He took her hand in his and turned on the cold water to irrigate to wound and see if she would need stitches. And she did. He grabbed a towel from off the counter and wrapped it tightly around her hand and began to usher her toward the front door and his car without asking her anything, including her permission.

He could see she was pale from shock and loss of blood. He became angry. What if he hadn't come back?, he thought. What if he had just gone back to his hotel? How could she be so stupid?

But he said none of these things to her as he drove her from Bell Park to Cabell Huntington's ER. He glanced over at her every few seconds and could see that she was not only faint, but also in a great deal of pain.

By the time the doctors had treated her hand and stitched up the four inch gash, he was allowed to go back to the curtained area where she lay upon an ER bed. As he entered the area, he saw that she was holding her bandaged left hand up with her right hand and was examining the bandages as if she might find something not right about it.

"I'm sure they've secured the bandages," Jack said.

Juls looked up at him and blinked for a moment. Was she even aware that he had been the person who had brought her here? He shook his head in disdain. She might not have the old Huntington Bell money, but she certainly had their air of superiority.

"Thank you, Jack," she said and cast her gaze back toward her hand. "I believe that you may have saved my life, or well, at least my hand."

He inhaled deeply before speaking.

"What were you thinking?" he asked.

She shrugged her shoulders. "I wasn't. That damned trunk was just driving me crazy. I had to see what was in it."

She looked up at him.

"Why did you come back?" She paused for a moment and tilted her head slightly. "You knew I couldn't leave it alone, didn't you?"

Jack nodded his head.

"I found a hacksaw in the basement and thought I could saw through the lock. I was holding the lock with my left hand and sawing with my right hand when the saw slipped and slid across my palm," she said.

Jack sat down at the edge of her bed as she replayed the events to him. He noticed that there was no icy reserve in her tone now. She was speaking low, in the tones of a conspirator, her voice barely loud enough for him to hear much less anyone else around. She leaned closer to him as she spoke and several times touched his hand with her right hand. Her skin felt soft and warm and he found himself distracted by her touch so much so that he was missing some of what she was telling him.

For the first time he felt a strong attraction to her and it made him very uncomfortable. She, or at least her family, was the subject of his book. It was unethical to allow himself to become too close to her. It could jeopardize his objectivity. It was wrong and he knew it, but the attraction was almost a tidal force as she leaned in toward him and he could smell the lavender scent of her shampoo emanating from her blonde hair as she spoke.

He pulled away from her and stood up, rubbing his forehead as if he had a headache, inching away from the bed and trying not to look at her.

"Will they be releasing you soon?" he asked.

She leaned back against the pillow and stared at the ceiling. There it was. The wall. It was up again. He had pulled away and she was now blocking him with an invisible wall of stubborn pride.

"Yes, but I can take a taxi home. No need for you to stay," she replied coldly.

"I'm here. I'll take you home. No reason to waste money on a cab," he said.

She shrugged as if to say "whatever" and rolled on her left side away from him, now using her body to physically block any interactions with him.

He smiled when she rolled away. Her attempt to block him failed more miserably than either of them could have dreamed. When she rolled away, the entirely of her back and legs was revealed to him thanks to the partially tied hospital gown. At least they had allowed her to retain her panties. He could not look away this time. The small dimple at the base of her spine, the tiny mole at the top of her right thigh, and her fine smooth skin were completely revealed to him.

Rather than just walk away though, he returned her modesty to her by taking the sheet at the end of the bed and raising it over her. She halfway turned back to him and pulled the sheet higher.

"Thank you," she said and blushed.

"No problem," he said and sat down in a hard blue plastic and metal chair at the foot of the bed. He watched her as she drifted off from the painkiller they had given her. Glancing at his wristwatch, he saw that it was now 1:30 a.m. He leaned his head against the wall behind him and closed his eyes. It was going to be a long night.

A nurse woke him two hours later as she was giving Juls her discharge instructions. He rubbed the sleep from his eyes and tried to quickly catch up with their conversation. Juls looked exhausted and limply signed her name to the release papers and instructions. The nurse put Juls's clothes on the bed and said as she was leaving the curtained room for Juls to return if the bleeding began again.

Juls lifted her shirt from the bed and saw that the blood had soaked it and left it unwearable. Her jeans weren't as bad and her sneakers were still fairly clean. But she discovered her largest problem was that she could do very little with her left hand that was bandaged as if she were wearing a partial Minnie Mouse glove.

Before she could decide what to try to do first, she found Jack kneeling in the floor in front of her with her jeans.

"Step in one leg at a time. Use your right arm to balance yourself against my shoulder," he said as he helped her into her jeans.

She stood and he, without looking up, zipped and buttoned the jeans for her.

"Sit back down and I'll get your shoes for you."

"What am I going to do about a shirt?" she asked. "I can't wear this. It's soaked."

He stood and walked toward the curtain. "Give me a minute."

He returned to her five minutes later with a blue denim shirt he had left in the back seat of his car.

"I know it's far too large, but you can wrap it around yourself and at least cover yourself."

He faced away from her as she removed the hospital gown and pulled his shirt around her smaller frame. As she struggled with the buttons, Jack picked up the bloody shirt and found her bra had been stuck inside it. He was holding the shirt in bewilderment when she appeared at his side and took the clothing in her right hand and threw the shirt and the bra into the trash can next to the bed.

"Can't be saved. Could you take me home now? Please?"

"Are they going to bring a wheelchair or something?" he asked.

"I don't know. I don't really care. I just want to get out of here," she said.

Fifteen minutes later she was in her own house and heading towards her bedroom at the rear of the house. Jack stood in the foyer, not quite sure whether to just go or wait and see if she needed anything else. He was just about to leave when she reappeared from the back of the house.

"I . . . This is embarrassing. I can't get the jeans unzipped. My hand is absolutely killing me and every time I move it, it hurts like hell,"

"Could you . . ."

"Yeah," Jack said. "Let me help you."

He followed her back to her bedroom and helped her remove the jeans, once again allowing her to retain her modesty by avoiding looking in her face. The silence between them was strong and he felt that tidal pull toward her again. He knew he had to leave the room.

He went to her kitchen and brought her a glass of water so she could take another pain killer. Just after turning her bedroom light off and closing her door, he heard her voice in the darkness..

"Jack, the other bedroom. You can stay in there if you want. It's almost dawn and you've got to be tired. We both need some rest."

She rolled on her side in the bed before he could reply, exhaustion overwhelming her.

He nodded yes, thinking after he nodded that she was probably unaware of his response. But as he closed the door again, he heard her quietly say "Thank you".

Chapter Seven

Summer 2010

When Jack awoke, he had the feeling of dislocation that he suffered from whenever he traveled to work on a book. Waking up in strange surroundings was disconcerting though he had been doing it for most of his adult life.

But this time, the silence was broken only by birdsong in the woods beyond her property. He had lain down on top of the comforter and had intended to only sleep for an hour or two, but he knew it had been longer. He looked around the room and realized that it had once been an enclosed porch. Two walls were solid banks of windows and bright sunshine filled the room with a pale yellow glow.

He sat up on the side of the bed and felt his back creak a bit. Another casualty of sleeping wherever he landed when he was working on a story, although this room was as good as the Ritz compared to the morning he had awakened on the beach in Indonesia after the 2006 tsunami.

He walked to Juls's bedroom first and was surprised to find it empty. He had expected to find Juls still sleeping after the trauma of last night. Instead, he found her in the dining room staring at the trunk.

"Good morning," he said.

She smiled good morning back at him and then returned her gaze to the trunk.

Jack waited for her to speak, but again she failed to speak.

"So, do you drink coffee or are you hungry?" he asked.

She shook her head as if trying to clear her thoughts and broke her gaze from the trunk.

"Oh, I'm sorry," she said, facing him. "Yes, I just hadn't gotten around to making anything. Actually, I hadn't thought of it yet." Then she looked down at her hand and frowned. "This is taking some getting used to."

She stole one more look at the trunk as if it would disappear and then rose to go to the kitchen.

"I can make the coffee, Juls. Just tell me where everything is," Jack said and then added, "Would you like some toast or something else as well? Let me do this for you. Rest your hand. If you don't, you'll regret it by the end of the day."

She smiled and said "Sure" and showed him around her kitchen, using her right hand to point at cabinets and the coffeemaker.

She suddenly laughed and said, "I feel like a "Price is Right" model, waving my one hand around. All we need is Drew Carey with a microphone." She leaned against the kitchen counter as if surveying how she would maneuver her way through the cabinets.

Jack laughed with her and began to make coffee and toast.

"You know, I just thought of a way of removing that lock," he said, then added, "Without a hacksaw."

She gave him a look that was supposed to look cross, but just ended up giving her a slightly sweet frown.

"A good hammer and a metal wedge. Think there might be one in your basement?" he asked.

"Yes, actually, I do know where they are. I can go get them now," she said and headed toward the basement stairs.

He barely managed to grab her right arm before she headed downstairs.

"Hold up there, speedy. After coffee and toast, you can show me where they are. Remember resting your hand? Now, go back to the dining room and I'll bring the coffee in there."

She nodded and walked away toward the dining room. Jack knew she was going back to the trunk. As he was buttering the toast, he leaned to the door and saw her back in her former position, sitting in the same chair, still staring at the trunk.

"You know you can't 'will' the lock to just open," he said as he brought the coffee and toast into the dining room.

"Of course, I know that, I'm not . . ." she stopped and saw the smile on his face.

"You are the most literal person I've ever met," Jack said.

She shook her head. "No, probably the most gullible," and she took a bite of the toast he had generously smothered in strawberry jam.

"Hardly. Gullible is never a word I would use to describe you. Impatient, maybe. But not gullible. No, definitely not gullible," he replied.

She sipped the coffee and returned her gaze to the trunk.

"I know this is going to sound ridiculously naïve, but I keep thinking that something in that trunk is going to make everything alright again."

Jack looked in her eyes and saw that she was absolutely serious. As he sipped his coffee, he thought she was more likely to be disappointed. He was afraid that this would be more like Al Capone's vault while she was hoping that something that would clear her family's name or perhaps the truth about her great-great grandmother's death was waiting there.

"I wouldn't raise my hopes too much," he said. "You're more likely to find Julia Bell's wedding dress in there or maybe just some other old clothes."

She nodded. He was right. But, he hadn't lived with the Bell name his whole life in a city as small as

Huntington. She knew that most people knew nothing of the murder and the scandal now, but every now and then someone like him would show up and dredge up the whole mess again.

Why was she talking to him, she asked herself.

Good god, she had even let him stay in her house last night and she had known him for all of three days. But then again, she had awoken in the hospital to find him sleeping in the chair next to her bed and that had given her a comfort she couldn't explain. She couldn't exactly explain why, not even to herself, but finding him there had made her feel better than she had in years.

"You're probably right. It's just that I grew up in this house and I never saw that little door, much less the trunk. Someone went to a lot of trouble to hide both and that seems suspicious. Either way, I suppose we'll find out soon enough," she said.

After finishing the toast and coffee, removing the dishes to the kitchen, and finding the hammer and wedge, they began to try to break the lock. Jack placed the wedge against the lip of the lock swung the hammer down hard. The lock didn't budge. Juls was starting to get tense. Jack swung again and this time the entire lock fell away from the trunk, the leather and wood behind the latch breaking into pieces.

Jack looked down at the mess and winced. "Sorry."

Juls paid no attention to him or the mess in the floor. She knelt down before the trunk and using her good hand, lifted the lid to the trunk. Nothing on earth could have prepared her for what she found.

"Wow" was all Jack could say. He was almost as surprised as she was.

Chapter Eight

January 25, 1937

Julia Chafin Bell had just finished a most unsatisfying breakfast. Too many people. Too much of McKenzie in this house and she found that odd in that he had never lived to see Thea grow up, marry, have children or live in this house.

Julia walked into the small solarium where Thea sat at a breakfast table re-reading the society pages of a newspaper printed before the flood. She sat down in a wicker rocker near her daughter.

"It simply amazes me, Mother, what this newspaper prints about these new families as if they were one of the first families of Huntington. Why, here's an article on Sarah Perry, as if she were someone important."

Julia sighed. She hated that Thea judged Sarah Perry on her background rather than her intelligence and kindness. Sarah was the wife of Julia's lawyer, Allen Perry, and was as far as she knew, a good wife and mother. Rather than pointing out to her daughter the obvious fact that Huntington was a growing city of new people and new ideas, she decided to ignore Thea's tirade and enquire about using Thea's driver and car.

"Thea, I have some errands to run today," she said. "Could your driver take me?"

Thea dropped the paper onto the table, paused a moment and then looked up and stared at her mother with her mouth hanging open.

"Do close your mouth, Thea. It is most unattractive," Julia said.

"Mother, you do realize the size of the tragedy that has befallen Huntington, don't you? Honestly, I believe your obstinacy will be the death of me. The roads are closed,

Mother. No one can go anywhere," Thea responded and noisily began to fold the paper up.

"Don't be overly dramatic, Thea. I've lived through five other floods without having to paddle a canoe. I sincerely doubt that this one will be any different."

Thea threw the paper onto the round wicker table.

"Mother, sometimes you are simply the most irrational person I have ever met," she said and stormed from the room.

Julia diverted her gaze from her feckless daughter and out toward the small back lawn of the home. In one corner a beautiful magnolia had been planted and its large leaves looked as if they could provide shelter from the continuing rain storm.

She breathed deeply and admitted to herself that Thea was most likely correct about this particular event. She had lived through so many floods from the Ohio, but this one did seem to be much more serious than any of the previous ones. And this was the first one that would find Huntington as a larger, modern and more complete city, rather than the collection of ramshackle wooden buildings that had housed most of the businesses in the past. The last floods had proved that brick and stone were far better building materials when facing a flood and those businesses that could rebuild in the past had done so avoiding wood except for interior details.

The few large homes that were left along Third Avenue past the railroad lines were homes such as hers that had been built of brick or stone as well. The other, smaller wooden ones had long since disappeared from the riverfront.

So, if she was stuck here in this house, what could she do? She refused to listen to that radio another second. Thea, never a reader of anything beyond the society pages, had very few books and the rain made any outdoor activities impossible. She wondered if any of the children had brought a deck of cards. Maybe a game of bridge or even a game of solitaire was better than sitting here looking at Thea's small backyard.

But instead of looking for a deck of cards, she returned to her bedroom and pulled from her valise a small leather bound journal she had kept since McKenzie had raped her on her second wedding night. She had dozens of them and each of them gave detailed accounts of her life, her dreams, fears, hatreds, and plans. She had just begun this one and had not written more than a few entries in it.

She began to write about the flood and her forced exit from her home, Thea's tiresome attitude, and her nephews who made her think that they might have inherited McKenzie's disturbed personality. She realized that they did nothing that did not benefit them, either directly or indirectly. She shuddered at the thought that McKenzie's evil bloodline had been sustained through her descendants. It didn't seem quite fair, she thought. She had had to endure McKenzie for so long and just as she was rid of him, she found him again in not one person, but in two of her own grandchildren. No, it wasn't fair. Not at all.

She closed the journal and returned it to its hiding place beneath the bottom lining of her valise. She had to get out of this house today to see her lawyer and she believed that one of those boys just might be her ticket out for at least a short period of time. She gathered her purse and coat and went through the house in search of one of them. She stood at the second floor landing and listened for their voices.

There. Upstairs. Of course, the third floor had become their pied a Terre when they were children and Thea could no longer afford to have live-in help. Julia had agreed to help Thea with a day maid, but she refused to pay for more than the maid and the driver. It was another crime for which Thea had never forgiven her mother. Thea conveniently forgot that her husband had abandoned her and she spent money as if she deserved it because she had been born a Bell. Julia thought that even if Thea knew the truth of Julia's life that she would still feel cheated.

As Julia began her ascent to the third floor, she could hear the echo of billiards cracking against one another and the laughter of the boys. She found Thea's sons there, but not Mack. She was not surprised. When the boys were young they tormented Mack, who was older than them and who could easily have stopped them but curiously enough did not and chose to avoid them and ignore their childish nonsense. Luckily, he had left for university before they would all attend Huntington High School together. And, although Julia had offered to pay for them to attend college, they chose not to do so, saying that they were planning on joining their father in Texas.

Julia knew this was a falsehood and that they would ask her for the college money in order to travel west, but she had no intention of giving them money that they would gamble away or spend on whores the way their father and grandfather had.

Kent saw her ascension into the third floor rooms before his brother, Reggie. Just as Reggie was about to start relating the story of the Smithson twins and their adventures on the Smithson family boat, Kent coughed loudly to signal to Reggie to stop and alert him to the presence of their grandmother. Reggie sneered and cast a sideways glance at his younger brother, but nevertheless stopped his story of his most enjoyable voyage on the Ohio with the twins.

"Grandmother, welcome to our gentlemen's room," Reggie said, greeting Julia with a bravado that she had not heard since McKenzie's death. She took a deep breath and tried not to show her utter distaste for her grandsons.

"Boys, I am in need of transportation. Your mother has said that it is impossible, but I find it an absolute necessity that I do make this short trip. I need one of you to take me to Allen Perry's home. As it is only a quarter mile from here and up the hill, I seriously doubt that the road there would be closed as your mother seems to think," she said.

Neither boy spoke, but both looked to the other. Disobeying their mother always carried consequences, but currying favor with their grandmother promised greater rewards. While Kent tended to agree with his mother that a trip out today was not a wise decision, he also thought of how his grandmother might repay this favor.

"Grandmother, I think Mother may be right in that we might not be able to cross Twelve Pole Creek on the other side of the park," Kent said, but before he could continue, Reggie had already stepped forward to take his grandmother's hand and volunteer his services as a chauffeur to her.

"Nonsense. We can never know unless we try, can we?" Reggie said. "Please allow me to drive you to Mr. Perry's home. If the roads are impassable, they will certainly be clear later."

Julia looked to Kent and wished he had not spoken negatively first. She would much rather prefer to spend the car trip with him than his brother.

Reggie not only possessed McKenzie's personality, but he also looked astonishingly like his grandfather and his mannerisms were just as similar. She nodded to Reggie in thanks for his offer.

"Very well, Reggie. I would like to leave immediately and I would like to do so without alerting your mother. I see no reason to disturb her with this errand," she said.

Kent placed the pool cue upon the table and watched as Reggie escorted their grandmother down the steps. Son of a bitch, he thought. By the time Reggie and Julia had descended to the first floor, Kent's anger had grown to the point that he took Reggie's cue stick and slammed it against the corner of the Brunswick billiards table, breaking it into splinters. One day, Reggie and the old bitch would pay. One day.

Meanwhile, Julia made her escape with Reggie without Thea's discovery of their absconding. She said little to nothing to Reggie in the car, although Reggie seemed not to notice her silence at all, continuing to chatter inanely about his friends and social life, seeming to forget the tragedy that was playing itself out in the downtown area.

When they reached the Perry home, she told Reggie to wait in the car and that she would return to him shortly. She was so glad to escape the confines of the car that she was tempted to tell him to return home without her had she not known that Thea would have sent him back to fetch her no matter what Julia's intentions were.

Perry's wife, Sarah, answered the door and Julia was rather surprised. She knew that they could afford at least one housemaid. Perhaps the girl had been unable to get there from downtown.

"Sarah, how are you today? I was hoping that Allen might be at home," Julia said, removing her gloves and coat and handing them over to the small woman standing before her.

Sarah Perry was astonished that Julia Bell had not only come out in this weather, but had actually come to her home and had known her name. Sarah and Julia traveled in completely different social circles. Sarah had moved to Huntington from Milton and often felt she was still regarded as a newcomer although she had now resided in the Park Hills for over 15 years now.

Julia's daughter, Thea, had made it clear that Sarah was not welcome in any of the Bell social circles, although Jonas Bell's wife had been quite welcoming. Nevertheless, Sarah thought that her family would have to be in Huntington for several generations before the likes of the Bell family would deign to involve themselves in her life. Little did she know that in less than a year that she would be the one needed for approval, that Thea's power would be ended as fast as her mother's life would be taken.

Sarah laid Julia's belongings on the hall chair and led the elderly woman into her front parlor where she seated her on a small blue and cream striped settee.

"I'll let Allen know that you're here immediately, Mrs. Bell. Would you like a cup of tea or coffee?" Sarah asked.

Julia smiled broadly, dropping her "grand dame" performance and said, "Please call me Julia, Sarah. And no, don't bother with anything. I wouldn't have interrupted your afternoon if it weren't an urgent business matter."

Sarah returned Julia's smile and left the room in search of her husband. He was upstairs with his young sons, playing with their tin soldiers with them on the floor of their bedroom. He was casually dressed and started to stop to put on a tie and vest before descending the stairs, but decided against it. If Julia Bell felt she could interrupt his family's afternoon in his own home, she would have to accept what she found, though knowing her nature better than most he didn't really see it as a problem.

"Julia, what a surprise," he said as he entered the parlor and rolled his sleeves down as he sat in a Chippendale chair upholstered in the same blue and cream stripe silk fabric as the settee.

"Allen, I would not have disturbed you at home, but I am greatly concerned about several matters and feel that I need to make changes to my will immediately. Is it possible to replace my current will without amending the previous one? Can I dictate a new one to you and have Sarah sign as a witness?"

Allen was struck by the urgency in Julia Bell's voice. She was not only in great haste to change the will, but she almost sounded fearful.

"Julia, has something happened? Are you in some sort of danger? This is very sudden."

"No, James, nothing but an old woman's weak fears. I probably should have waited until next week," she said and looked down at her hands.

"Julia, I can certainly make any changes you wish. I could even do it today if it's simple, but anything complicated will require much more time. You do have a very large estate," he said, leaning towards her, trying to calm whatever fears she might be harboring.

"Allen, it's a very simple change. I wish to disinherit my entire family. They are to receive nothing beyond what they have already received from me. I assume that since McKenzie's sudden death left everything in my hands that there should be no complications from that arena," she said and smiled.

Chapter Nine

January 25, 1937

That night Allen Perry was unusually silent at dinner and Sarah knew that it had to do with Julia Bell's appearance at their home that afternoon. While she had discreetly found chores to do in other parts of the house, she could not help but hear some of the conversation that had gone on between her husband and Mrs. Bell.

She was as astonished as Allen that Julia Bell was disinheriting her family. She had heard that one bit of information quite clearly. It would certainly have an impact on how the Bells would react to her when they saw her in public and it worried her that it might not be a positive thing for her family.

Thea Bell Harris had for some unfathomable reason made it her mission to abuse Sarah and Allen as often as possible. Perhaps it was because Thea assumed that Sarah knew something about the Bell family because Allen was Julia's lawyer, but Thea was very mistaken. With the exception of this afternoon's visit, Sarah knew nothing about Allen's business or his clients. He was completely circumspect in his legal matters and Sarah was actually very glad he was. She had no desire to know the personal or financial aspects of people in Huntington.

As Sarah cleared the table of the supper dishes, she did wish that Addie were here to help her today. Julia Bell had been correct in her assumption that Sarah's housemaid was unable to get to the Perry home because of the flood. When Sarah finished carrying the last of the dishes to the kitchen sink, she felt guilty about feeling inconvenienced by Addie's absence. She knew that Addie lived in an apartment on 4th Avenue and 5th street and that the flood waters could very well have reached Addie's home, but she had no way of knowing for sure. There was no phone service and most of the electrical service for the city beyond the railroad had also been affected. She couldn't even try to drive to Addie's as she had no idea of how far inland the flood waters had reached. She would have brought Addie and her family here to stay and silently berated herself for not thinking of that earlier.

As she filled the sink with hot water, she felt both relief and guilt over her own good fortune and the misfortunes of those who lived in other parts of town. She could hear her sons listening to the radio with James in the parlor and she looked out the kitchen window and wondered if the rain were going to stop anytime soon. It seemed as if the constant rain was just one more ill omen of bad times to come.

Allen Perry's mind was on other matters entirely. The flood was no longer something that preoccupied his mind. Julia Bell had changed that with her short visit this afternoon. Disinheriting her family would not mean immediate problems for him other than simple clerical chores and those future problems were not a pleasant thought. The rest of the Bell family would attack him with everything they could muster, that is if they had the money to mount such an attack and he could not be sure of that.

He knew a few things about Jonas's business and he knew almost everything about Thea's finances and those of her sons. He did not relish a confrontation with any of these people.

Jonas and his family may well be tolerable in any dealings, but Thea and her two monstrous sons were another matter entirely.

While she might prove difficult in some legal aspects, most of her anger would be toothless, yet vituperative attacks on his wife and family. The sons presented a different problem.

Julia was afraid of someone or something and Allen believed that those boys were at the heart of her fear. They had been spoiled and mean young boys who had grown into sophisticated and dangerous young men. If they discovered that Julia has disinherited their mother or them, they might be physically vindictive to him and his family.

Why had Julia decided to do this, he wondered. He could understand leaving Thea and her useless sons nothing, but he could not understand why she would do this to Jonas. Jonas, as far as she had ever discussed with him, had always been a good and caring son. Julia liked Jonas's wife and their son. It simply made no sense unless there were threats she had seen from them all of which he knew nothing.

There was also one other possibility. Julia was almost 79. She could be mentally unwell. She could be seeing threats that did not exist at all. He sat back in the armchair next to radio and sighed as his boys played in the floor. How sad if she were becoming senile, he thought. She was such an incredible woman, with superior intellect, grace, and strength, especially in the face of what he had heard about her life with her husband, McKenzie. McKenzie had been a horror of a husband and, from everything he had been told, Julia had been lucky to see him die early.

Now, he was afraid that her death could mean great problems for him and his family, challenges that could be

Chapter Ten

Summer 2010

Jack looked at Juls's face and could see that what they had found was not what she had expected. The trunk was packed with small journals. Hundreds of them. He wanted to pick one of them up and start reading, but this was Juls's birthright, not his. He could see the disappointment on her face mixed with confusion and maybe apprehension.

Each journal looked to be about five inches by seven inches in size and almost all of them leather bound. Without touching them, he could see that red rot had found a home among some of them and he worried that silverfish or roaches might have eaten their way through them as well. At the very least, he felt that there was probably foxing on many of the pages.

He thought about preservation of them before they began to go through them and so he touched Juls gently on the shoulder to bring her back to the present. She looked up at him and he saw her eyes were brimming with tears.

He had definitely not expected this. Juls had not seemed to him to be someone who cried easily. She had nearly split her hand in two last night and she had not shed a single tear. Her stoicism throughout the past three days had never have prepared him for this.

"Juls, are you ok?" he asked quietly.

She wiped her eyes with her right hand and sniffed back the tears.

"Of course, yes, I just never thought we'd find a trunk full of old books. Letters, maybe. Even clothing. But books? Why would someone fill this with all these rotting books?" she asked.

Jack realized that she did not comprehend that these weren't just old books and he took one from the top of the stack and opened it. They were just as he thought –

journals, some probably over a hundred years old and he was willing to bet that they were all written by one person.

"Juls, these aren't just books. They're journals. Here, look," he said and handed the book to her.

She looked at the open book and saw the copperplate handwriting there and the date at the top of the page and then looked back at him.

"My god, do you think they're all the same?"

Jack shrugged.

"Probably. Maybe one person's entire life. I don't think you'll know until you start going through them."

As he was speaking, Juls flipped through the pages of the book and lost her handhold on it. As the book fell to the floor next to her, it seemed that they watched in slow motion as paper money flew into the air, dislodged from the pages of the journals. Next to where the book landed were three crisp $1,000 dollar bills.

Jack and Juls looked at each other in astonishment again. Jack picked up the one of the bills and saw it was a $1,000 bill, dated 1934. It was crisp and absolutely flawless as if it had just been minted.

"What the hell?" he said, turning the $1,000 bill over in his hand. He picked up the other bills and saw that there were sequential serial numbers listed on each of them. He then picked up the book and began to gently leaf through the pages of the journal. By the time he had finished going through the book, he had found twenty, crisp 1934 $1,000 bills in just the one book.

Juls grabbed another book and was not as careful as Jack had been and began pulling money from it as well.

"Jack, my god Jack, why? Who did this? And why didn't my grandfather take this money and use it? He had to have been the one who put the trunk there, unless . . ."

"Oh no, surely not," she didn't bother to finish her sentence looking to him in both puzzlement and fear.

Jack stood and helped her to her feet and sat her down on one of the dining chairs. She was shaking.

"Juls, we need to do this slowly. First, we need to find out if the money is real. Then we need to go through each of the journals and see if there is more money in them as well."

"We need to read the journals, or at least you do, since they belong to you. And we should probably get some sort of fireproof lockbox to put the money in until you can get a safe deposit box. We can't just leave this money out in your house."

"There's a lot for you to do here. Perhaps you should call your parents. This is your family's heritage and I'm not sure that I'm the one who should help you with this task," he continued.

Juls shook her head. "No, I need you to help me with this, especially reading the journals. My father has had to deal with this too much. He's had too much pain because of whatever really happened in the past. I don't think he would even want to look at these journals."

"And," she went on, "I read a lot, but this is more than I can handle and with my hand out of commission . . . Please, I need your help and I need your discretion. Besides, you brought this mess into my life."

He nodded his head. "Well, the answers to some of your family's mysteries could be here, including the disappearance of the family money."

Juls stiffened and remembered that Jack's initial reason for being here was his "investigation" of her great-great-grandmother's murder and the scandal of the Bell family. Did she really want his help, after all?

Jack saw the wavering emotions on her face and knew immediately what she was thinking. He reached across the dining table and took her right hand in his.

"I promise not to use this if you don't want me to do so. I can always go back to the Collis Huntington book or find some other topic elsewhere," he said.

She looked down at his hand touching hers and shook her head. "Let's just take it a step at a time. I don't even know what we've got here."

She paused and furrowed her brow for a moment.

"I wonder if Marshall Media has archival boxes? We need archival tissue or envelopes and boxes for the journals," she said.

"Marshall Media?" Jack asked.

"Yes, it's an art and educational supply store over near Marshall University. They may carry archival supplies," she replied.

Jack stood and replaced the two journals they had removed back into the trunk and closed the lid. He winced again at the damaged lock. They could certainly use it now.

"If you feel like going out, let's go try to find the supplies we need for this project and get started," he said.

She smiled and nodded. "Yes, let's go now."

Chapter Eleven

Summer 2010

Jack and Juls first went to Marshall Media and found that the store did carry the basic archival supplies they needed. Juls bought three large boxes for the journals, two hundred acid free paper document sleeves into which each journal could be inserted, as well as archival pens to mark the sleeves and a ream of acid free paper in case they needed to make notes to include with each of the journals.

Jack recommended to her that they buy cotton gloves to handle the "items" as he phrased it in the store and she bought a box of cotton gloves with tiny raised dots on the fingertips to help handle the books carefully.

They then went to Wal-Mart and bought a small fireproof lockbox safe in which to place the money. They discussed in the car how they could bundle the money using strips they could cut from the acid free paper. They could decide later in what amounts to bundle the bills once they found out if there were more in the other books and whether they should bundle the bills in sequential order whenever they appeared that way.

Their final stop was at a coin collector's shop in Barboursville. Juls knew of them and had heard that they had a good reputation for giving honest appraisals. Jack and Juls had brought two bills with then without sequential serial numbers to have the bills appraised. Neither of them was surprised to discover that the bills were indeed genuine, although they were very surprised to find out that each bill was worth more than triple the face value.

The owner of the store explained that they were more valuable because they were of the A series from 1934 and that they carried a probable grade of about 50 to 60 since they were in the "About Uncirculated" class.

Jack and Juls looked confused at his terminology and he explained to them the importance of the bills.

"A grade of 50 to 60 is used by collectors that basically means that these bills look as if they came straight from the bank. They've been well protected and unhandled. Treasury stopped making them after the beginning of World War II and they were taken out of circulation in the early 1960s. There are probably only about 165,000 of these bills left in private hands according to the US Treasury, so that makes them more desirable to collectors," the shop owner told them.

"I have collectors who would jump at the chance to have one of these in this kind of condition," he said and offered them $1750 on the spot for each bill.

"Are they still legal tender?" Jack asked.

The owner said yes, but they really should consider selling them to collectors rather than taking them to a bank.

Juls smiled and thanked the owner and offered to pay him for his appraisal, but he declined, only asking that if they decided to sell them that they think of him first. They agreed that if they decided to sell them that they would do just that.

By the time she and Jack had finished their errands, they were ravenous and Juls suggested the China Garden restaurant on the corner of Eighth Street and Sixth Avenue.

"I've been eating there since I was a child and their food is wonderful. Not to mention that I'm not going to be very useful in the kitchen for a while," she said.

Jack said it sounded great and he was just relieved to sit down for awhile and get out of Huntington traffic. Saturday evening traffic turned into a nightmare with the residents of three states and the student population of Marshall University converging on the downtown area.

Huntington had surprised him in many ways. He had heard horror stories in the national media about it being one of the worst places in the country in which to live, but he found it was actually a very beautiful city with friendly people. He was very surprised by the Ritter Park area where great numbers of people seemed to do everything from walk in the beautiful rose gardens to jog the length of the park that seemed to be at least several miles long.

The park itself was a beautiful gift to the residents of the city. Lush with blooming trees and flowers, the park contained beautiful sculptures, play areas for children, a great running path, sidewalks and hiking trails, an amphitheater where concerts were held throughout the summer, a plethora of tennis courts, and small bridges over a clean, small creek that ran the length of the park.

The people there were also quite literate and completely unrepresentative of the stereotypes pasted upon them by the outside media. They were a bit provincial, but what small city wasn't, he thought. And he liked the fact that they could walk through the city at night in relative safety. There were a lot of cities in which he had stayed of which he could not say the same.

From his research he knew that most of Huntington had been planned as a modern 20th century city, although it was not incorporated until 1871. Collis Huntington's people had hired an architect to design the town with broad thoroughfares, residential and business zones, and parks, although Mr. Huntington had reneged on the money for the parks after achieving his initial goals for the railroad. He moved on and left the city that bore his name to its own devices. Luckily for Huntington, the intelligent men who had been the farmers from whom Collis Huntington had bought most of the railroad land stepped up and continued with the vision of a beautiful city on the shores of the Ohio.

With the exception of a few areas that grew from later development at the eastern and western edges of the city, they succeeded, including the building of a superb educational system and molding Marshall Academy, first built in 1837, into Marshall College. Jack thought that they would be proud of the fine university that Marshall had become, with some of the campus buildings bearing the names of those early men.

Jack knew that had it not been for the tragedy of her great-great grandmother's murder, her family's name would be just as prominent in city lore. Unfortunately, the murder had wiped her family's name from almost everything except the small development where she lived.

He thought of how the Egyptians had removed the names of rulers when they were deposed or died and scandal followed. He allowed himself a small inward smile at the coincidence of how the Bell scandal was handled in a similar manner. Perhaps, it was best for Juls. He imagined that her grandfather, father, and other family members had paid dearly for Julia Bell's murder, no matter who the perpetrator may have been.

He and Juls sat quietly through most of the meal, each of them thinking of the discoveries they had made since last night. Jack looked across the table at Juls and saw a very beautiful woman to which his resistance was failing fast. Something about her kept drawing him towards her no matter how much he fought it. It wasn't that he hadn't cared about the people he had written about or worked with before, but this was different. She was different. She was one who stood apart from them in a way he couldn't articulate yet and it made him a little crazy that he couldn't find the words to describe the feelings she evoked in him. She frustrated and fascinated him at the same time, but there was something beyond that. He knew it. He just couldn't put a name to it yet.

Chapter Twelve

Diary of Julia Priscilla Chafin
June 17, 1876

Tomorrow I shall write my first entry in this diary as Julia Priscilla Chafin Bell! I am both apprehensive and excited about tomorrow's planned events. I cannot believe that such a handsome, well figured and intelligent man wishes to marry me, but I do so despair at the thought of leaving my family home. How I will miss both my parents and my dear brother, Christopher.

Everyone around me continues to tell me what a wonderful match I have made, and I do believe I will love Mr. Bell, but becoming a married woman carries such responsibilities with it. I fear he may find that I may fall short in many areas. I can only pray that I can be the good wife for him that the gracious Lord will help me to be.

So many plans have been made for the wedding. We are going to have a wedding portrait made by Thornton Barrette, a very well known local photographer.

Mr. Bell has insisted that a proper society wedding should be recorded for posterity and that notices of our wedding, including details of all aspects of the nuptials as well as our honeymoon plans be printed in the *Huntington Argus*. I was quite surprised on his insistence on these details as many of my friends have not had such public weddings, but Mr. Bell said that in "polite" society such events would occupy more than just a society note of a few sentences as most newspapers outside of the larger cities carry.

Either way, I would be agreeable to his plans as he is a worldly man and knows much more about such things than I would know. He has seen to the smallest details, including ordering the most beautiful ivory silk and tulle for my wedding clothes as well as the engraved invitations shipped here all the way from Baltimore.

He also surprised me with the location of our honeymoon. I had expected something modest at first and then began to envision Baltimore, but no, Mr. Bell is taking me to Chicago for our honeymoon. Just imagine! I have never travelled farther than Charleston and that was a stagecoach journey that took two days. Now I will be travelling by train in a private car that Mr. Huntington has granted us the use of as a wedding gift! I can only dream of the wonders which I will see in such a great city.

I must end my writing for the evening. I hear dear mother mounting the stairs, no doubt with more advice and information about my nuptials tomorrow!

Chapter Thirteen

Diary of Julia Priscilla Chafin Bell
June 19, 1876

How do I begin to describe my first 24 hours of married life? I have prayed many times during the past day for guidance and I often wish my mother were here to advise me.

I have failed as a wife. I believed that I had done everything correctly. I was good and obedient and warm and yet the minute we left on the train, as we were waving good-bye to family and friends, Mr. Bell became distant and cold. I was most circumspect in my behavior and having had my mother tutor me on what to expect on my wedding night, I felt myself prepared for our union as man and wife.

After we entered our rail car, Mr. Bell left to another part of the train immediately. I thought that this might be because he was being considerate of my innocence, but after waiting for most of a very long night for his return, I fell asleep in our marriage bed. When he did return at 2 a.m., he was quite inebriated and disheveled. He still did not speak to me and simply threw himself on top of the bed fully clothed where he passed out, unmindful of me or the importance of last night.

This morning when I awoke I found him again gone from the car. I dressed and rang for a steward to bring me breakfast and while I ate I wondered whether I should try to find him on the train.

I thought of my mother's words about a man's strong will and hatred of a nagging or clinging wife so I spent the rest of today in the car reading and watching the scenery of the farmland as the train passed through it.

I was preparing for bed again this evening, still not having heard or seen Mr. Bell today when he finally appeared at our bedroom door. He was again drunk and I was beginning to become afraid that I would never become a true wife when he without warning savagely attacked me, slamming me face down upon the bed and ripping my nightclothes away in the full light.

I was initially very embarrassed by my nakedness, but when I realized his intentions, I tried to turn myself to him as a good wife should. That was when he slapped me hard against my ear and threw me back into my previous position.

The entire time these events were transpiring I was pleading with him to be gentle with me. When he pushed himself into me, he muffled my scream by wrapping his hand around my head and over my mouth. He hit me several times more and his member was rammed repeatedly into me with extreme force. I wept as he finished with me and realized that there was a great amount of my blood upon the bedclothes as he buttoned his trousers.

"I knew you were clean, but now you're not. Guess you won't be feeling so superior to me now," he said and began to laugh as he staggered away from the bedroom and toward the door to the rest of the train.

I wept copious tears as I lay in pain upon the bed. My mother had told me that my husband might be somewhat rough, but it was sometimes the way of men and that as an obedient, Christian wife, I should submit to his desires.

As I write this now, I do not believe that what occurred tonight was about what she was speaking. I believe that were he not my husband, he would be called my rapist for there was no love or gentility or husbandry about what he did to me. My body aches horribly and my heart feels broken. I do not believe he will return again tonight so after replacing the bloody bedclothes and my torn nightgown and washing myself as well as I could, I have taken the time to write this down and then will hide this journal under the lining of my traveling trunk.

I am so frightened and confused. Is this the way married life, at least the most intimate part of it, is to be? I pray to our heavenly father that Mr. Bell will not be so cruel to me again and that I can be deserving of his love.

I must discover how I have failed him for surely it is my fault as a wife that this terrible night has occurred. I will pray more after going to bed for the Lord's guidance for I fear I am an unworthy wife at this time.

Chapter Fourteen

Diary of Julia Chafin Bell
June 25, 1876

We have been in Chicago for several days now, but I have yet to see anything beyond the walls of our hotel room except what I spied from the window of the coach that carried us from the train to the hotel.

Looking out the hotel window, it seems to be a very large and crowded place, with the streets teeming with people of all types milling about or walking briskly toward destinations unknown to me.

My husband has continued his nightly torture. Each night the pain had eased somewhat, but it is still nothing for what my mother had prepared me. He curses me throughout our intercourse and often hits me without any provocation. Once I tried to plead with him for him to explain why he was hitting me, but it was a horrible mistake. It angered him further to the point that he threw me against the wall, pinning me there like a butterfly impaled in place not by a pin, but by his member.

His only comment to me during these nightly torture sessions has been to instruct me to lie face down upon the bed, unclothed and to bury my face into the pillow. He said he could not bear to see my "ugly visage" or hear my "shrill voice" so I have endeavored to do exactly as he says rather than be beaten about the head.

Some of the bruises on my face have faded in the past week. It is only the new ones he inflicts upon my body that would be seen were I not wearing modest attire.

How can I describe the horrors to which he has forced me to submit? If I were to describe it to anyone, I am sure that they would think me mad. One night he, God help me, he used his cravats to tie my arms to the bedposts and spread my legs apart, also tying my feet to the foot posts of the bed. I was terrified at this point and I believed that he might actually murder me, but instead he pushed pillows under belly and raised my buttocks from the bed.

Several minutes passed and I was shivering in fright, but remained silent. It was when he took one of my handkerchiefs and balled it up into my mouth, securing it with another scarf, did I begin to whimper.

It was only when I felt his member at my nether regions that I realized that he intended to molest me again, but nothing prepared me for what he did at that point. Instead of placing himself where a man would normally insert himself, he pushed himself into my rear opening and began pounding himself over and over. I knew then why he had completely silenced me as the pain was so excruciating that I thought I would die from it. I could feel my skin tearing again and I began to struggle to escape his assault. Those movements only made him push himself harder and faster into me until he fell forward upon me having finally exhausted his lust.

I had hoped that once we arrived in Chicago that the situation would change and that he would once more be the man who courted me so that I could show him what a good wife I was, but after that night I knew he was not the husband I had been told he would be and that what he had done to me was done of hate and disgust. We will never truly be a loving husband and wife. I will be strong even when he hurts me, but I will never forgive or forget how he has tormented me. I am disgusted by him and by myself for allowing his attacks, but what choice do I have? God help me, I would end my life if I were a stronger woman for no godly woman would be the object of such obscenities.

My one solace is that he disappears each day and only returns at night to hurt me and curse me.

I thought at first that I must be a wretched wife and a horrible embarrassment to him, but I now know that this hatred exists within him and is not because of me. If this is to be my fate, it may not be one I can suffer. I am so despondent and I implore God each night to help me understand my failings and what I have done to deserve this punishment.

Chapter Fifteen

Summer 2010

Juls had just finished reading the first entries in her great-great grandmother's first journal when she felt the contents of her stomach lurching upward. She threw the journal upon the table where she and Jack were working and ran to the bathroom, barely getting the door shut before allowing her dinner to heave into the toilet bowl.

Once the heaving stopped. She leaned back against the cool aqua tile and wept for her poor, poor grandmother. It was not enough that she had been murdered, but to have been placed in an arranged marriage with a sadist who brutally raped her continually was just too much for Juls to consider. Poor Julia. From the age of 17 she had been doomed to a life of physical torture and eventual murder, possibly at the hands of her own son.

Juls thought of being descended from such monsters and her stomach threatened to send her to the toilet again, but she managed to maintain control. She could hear Jack standing outside the bathroom door.

"I'm ok. Just give me a few minutes," she said to him through the closed door. She could hear him pause a moment and then heard his footsteps returning to the dining room. Since their discovery of the journals and the money, they had both spent days sorting through the journals and placing them in chronological order. Jack had taken on the task of counting and sorting the money while Julia took the first journal and had just begun to read it after placing the 227 slender volumes into dated and numbered sleeves.

Juls was so grateful for Jack's help, but now looking into the mirror she barely recognized herself and saw only the terrible men who had been her grandfathers. How could Jack ever look at her and not be disgusted by the family who had brought her into this world? Their evil blood flowed in her veins and she began to quietly weep.

Jack had been staying in the back bedroom while they worked on the contents of the trunk. He had been a good housemate with a quick wit and easy laugh. She had not realized just how lonely she had been until she began to awaken and look forward to hearing his voice in the kitchen in the morning.

She had taken one month's leave of absence from work, part of it medical and part of it vacation time she had accumulated and never used. Schulte, her boss, had asked her to make it a shorter period, but she told him that she had to have at least two weeks before she could use her left hand again and that she did not want to risk causing further damage so she was going to use some of her vacation time, too. It was just as well. She didn't think she could return to work now or anytime soon anyway.

She did not know whether she felt more disgusted by being the descendant of McKenzie and Jonas Bell or more heartbroken for her poor tortured grandmother's soul. Wiping a washcloth across her face, she allowed its coolness to soothe her eyes. Just as she was doing this, she remembered that she had left the journal on the table and that Jack had probably gone into the dining room and was reading it now.

She threw the cloth down and threw the bathroom door open, walking quickly back into the dining room where Jack indeed was sitting and reading the journal. She stopped at the door facing and watched him as he looked up from the journal to see her standing there. Without speaking, he closed the journal, placed it on the table and moved to where she stood, placing his arms around her shoulders and holding her.

"You cannot change what she went through and you cannot take on her pain or their guilt. It happened over 135 years ago," he said.

She clasped his chest with her arms and buried her face in his chest, sobbing so hard that her body shook. It seemed as if time stopped at that point. When she began to allow the sobs to recede, she looked up into his eyes. He bent forward and placed his mouth tentatively against hers as if unsure how she would respond.

She felt his soft and gentle kiss build her own desire and she responded with a strong and deep kiss. Their embrace began to move beyond mere kisses and he lifted her from the floor and carried her to the back bedroom where he had been sleeping and laid her upon the antique quilt. He paused and looked at her, silently questioning whether this was what she wanted.

Juls responded again by pulling him down to her and kissing him as she removed his white polo shirt and stroked the broad musculature of his chest and shoulders. As he removed the rest of his clothing, she, too, undressed quickly. She began pulling her t shirt over her head, but found herself struggling to remove her jeans, still having to deal with her wounded hand.

Jack stopped her and took her left hand and kissed her fingers lightly as he unzipped her jeans with his other hand. He slid the jeans from her legs and quickly removed her bra and panties just as effortlessly. He stopped for a moment and took in the beauty of her full breasts and long legs, the smooth skin with no sign of tan lines, the freckles that dotted her collarbone and how her blonde hair spread across the pillow framing the fine features of her face.

She removed his glasses and looked into his deep brown eyes for the first time without fear or defensiveness and saw something there that the dark glasses hid – he was a handsome man who wore the glasses like a disguise. She thought momentarily of Clark Kent and laughed and understood for the first time why no one could see Superman in Kent. Jack was superlative in his disguise of being an ordinary man when his eyes told her he was one of the most extraordinary men she had ever met.

Their bodies joined together almost immediately in a joyous movement of lovemaking. They spent hours that evening discovering everything they could about one another and each other's bodies with the waning light of the sun shining a beacon that led them unabashedly toward an unknown future that neither of them could understand, but she now saw that she could face, unafraid.

Later, only as the sun was beginning to set and the light in the room was beginning to dim did they only begin to talk to one another openly, without reservation. Juls told Jack of her fears of what her family bloodline might hold and that she was terrified that such evil ran in her family and that she might carry it within her.

Jack told her that her fears were baseless and that she was not the product of either McKenzie's misogyny or Jonas's addiction. He pointed out to her that she was so much stronger than most women he had known in his life and that even her great-great grandmother had been strong enough to survive 78 years. He told her that she carried that strength within her and that Julia would find her an amazing woman.

They talked long into the night and fell asleep at some point in one another's arms, each of them trying to forget everything that had led them to this moment in this bed, only thinking of their need for one another.

As Jack closed his eyes, he thought about the fact that he had broken every rule he had set for himself when writing about someone and he realized that he did not care. He softly kissed Juls's eyelids and lay back on the pillow, allowing sleep to overtake his exhausted body.

But for Juls, the komodo dragons returned to her dreams that night. She had thought that with their discovery of the trunk and the journals that the dragons would disappear from her dreams, but she was wrong. This night they were closer than they had ever been and she could smell their fetid bodies as the formed a tight circle around her. This time they had her frozen in place and she began to scream as one lunged at her on the bright white sand of the beach.

Jack grasped her in her sleep, shaking her from the dream.

"Juls. Juls, wake up. It's ok. You're ok. You're safe," he said, holding her tightly against his chest.

She struggled to control herself and to surface from the dream as if she were swimming upward through water toward a light that seemed impossibly distant. When she finally woke up, she found that she was panting, her breath coming fast and hot against Jack's chest. She realized the dragons would never leave, thinking that they were in her now and that she could never escape them and that she would never sleep again.

She looked up to Jack's face and into his eyes in the dim light from the streetlamps outside the house.

"She will never know peace," she said to him. She left unsaid the thought that she would never know peace again either. She rolled away from him and onto her back, staring at the shadows of the tree branches that seemed to etch their shapes against the ceiling.

No matter what happy endings or ideas of heaven anyone could think of for the poor victims of torture and murder such as her grandmother, she knew deep within herself that it was a grievous lie that people told themselves in order to continue to live with the knowledge that such evil walked among them every day.

Juls thought that there was no justice for those women, just a painful and empty death where they disappeared first from the lives of those around them and then from the earth itself. Eventually even the memory of them disappeared and no one was left to mark the fact that they had walked the earth or that they had loved and lived and breathed. In the end, they simply became forgotten and were only sometimes left as a footnote in the story of their killer.

She closed her eyes and rolled away from Jack. What good would any of this do anyone? Even the money was tainted by the obscenities of what Julia endured. None of it mattered. It all just evaporated into the steam that would feed someone else's idea of what life should be.

Jack watched as Juls pulled away from him and reached his hand out to touch her shoulder blade, his hand hovering above it for a second before he withdrew it. He wasn't sure why, but he knew she couldn't suffer anyone's touch right now, not even his, and he felt a great sadness fall over him.

Chapter Sixteen

Summer 2010

Jack awoke in the bed alone, as if Juls had never been there. He sat up and rubbed the sleep from his eyes, grabbing his glasses from the night stand and looked around the room. He had never felt so alone and out of place in his life. How such a beautiful night could have ended so lonely and sad, he wondered.

He kept going back to the things they had said to one another last night. He knew that it all had to do with Juls's own ideas and perceptions of who she was and of those from whom she had come. He had found himself just as shocked as she had been by the torture of her then 17 year old great-great grandmother, but he had to find a way for Juls to accept that she was not the end result of that horrible beginning. He believed that time would be the only way for Juls to reconcile herself to what had happened and he considered the possibility that she might withdraw into that defensive posture she carried around herself.

After dressing, he found her back in the dining room. She had more of the journals out. They were strewn haphazardly across the table in front of her. Their protective sleeves tossed to the side, some even lying in the floor next to where she sat as if she had just dropped them there. She did not look up to him when he entered the room and he waited for a few moments, started to speak, then stopped himself and turned to the kitchen in search of coffee and something to eat.

He wanted to pull the journals from her hands and drag her from the house, do anything to get her away from Julia's legacy. Part of him was angry that Julia had left those journals for her children or grandchildren to read, but the objective side of him told him that Julia had felt it important for them to be kept and found. They carried a dual legacy – both the money and the truth of her life that no one had really known.

And the money, well, the money could help Juls leave this place where she was finding nothing but pain. He had estimated that with just the face value of the bills, Juls had just inherited over 4.5 million dollars. If he added the collector's value to the money, the value could go up to almost 9 million. Even if she gave half of the money to her dad and mom, she'd still be quite well off.

As Jack made coffee he realized that he had not taken into account the rest of Juls's family. Were there other descendants out there besides Juls and her dad? He tried to remember the terms of Julia's will and Jonas's for that matter, although he was almost positive that there were no other living descendants of Jonas other than Juls and her dad.

He did remember that Julia's daughter, Thea, had had two sons. What were their names? Reggie and Kent. He searched his memory for any names that might have been descendants of them but blanked on them.

He would have to check that stupid family history book to see if the men had had children. And Juls, either she or her father would have to retain a lawyer. This amount of money made it all much more complicated than he had ever expected when he had knocked on Juls's door last week.

Walking back into the dining room, he placed a cup of coffee on the table next to Juls and sat down across from her, waiting. Had it only been a week? He shook his head and looked at the mess the dining room had become. Boxes and envelopes and journals were everywhere and that didn't take into account the money that sat in the fireproof safe under the table. They really needed to get that to a safe deposit box as soon as possible.

"Juls," he said.

She started to turn another page in the journal she was reading, but she stopped and laid it upon the table in front of her and picked up the coffee and began to drink it all the while staring at him as if his sex alone made him evil.

"How long have you been up reading," he asked.

She placed the cup on the table, looked out the window and sighed. She knew she was being unfair to him, but she felt that what had happened last night had been a mistake of enormous proportions. She should never have let him know about any of this. He was an outsider and she had stupidly allowed him access to everything, including herself.

She had grown up knowing that protecting herself and her family because of the legacy of Jonas's infamy was paramount to her existence and she had failed. Not only had she failed, she thought, but she had made it worse by allowing him to know what sort of man McKenzie Bell had been. She did not believe that Julia had intended for anyone other than a family member to read those journals.

She turned back to Jack. His face showed only concern. Perhaps she was being too hard on both of them. Perhaps not.

"I've read through the first ten years of Julia's life with McKenzie. It was not an easy decade for her," Juls said, failing to add that the reading had not been easy for her, either.

McKenzie had continued his punishing sexual and emotional torture of Julia for a part of those ten years, with the sexual torture only concluding after she had conceived their first child, Jeremiah, three years later. After Jeremiah's birth, McKenzie stopped coming to her and began habiting the bordellos on Second Avenue on the western end of town.

Jack sipped his coffee in silence. He didn't know what to say to Juls. At this point, he just wanted shed of the whole matter. He looked at her and could not believe that last night had meant nothing to her. It made him angry and hurt. He had thought that they had shared something wonderful and she acted as if it had never happened.

"Juls, I'm thinking I might leave. I don't know that I'm doing any good for you now and, well, perhaps it's better if I left."

He stood and looked down her emotionless face. He winced slightly when he thought he saw in her face that she wanted him gone.

"You can take care of the rest of this. You don't need me," he said extending his arms outward. He had expected more of a reaction from her.

Juls inhaled sharply, her nostrils flaring slightly.

"It's easy to just leave," she said. "I'll never understand how men can always just walk away and not look back. You came in here and opened up this mess and now you decide to just leave. Well, ok. Go. Go." She stood herself and threw what was left of the contents of her coffee cup in his face, leaving the room with him standing there, a sodden mess.

Jack was stunned. He wiped the coffee from his face and then followed her through the house. When he reached her at her bedroom door, he grabbed her left arm and twirled her around to face him.

"What the fuck is wrong with you? You act as if I'm the enemy or worse, one of your fucking ancestors. I came here to write a story".

"You *asked* for my help with that damned trunk. You *asked* for my help with the journals and the money," he said, omitting the part about her complete disassociation from any intimacy they had shared yesterday.

He looked down and saw that her face was white with fear and let go of her arm. He backed away from her a step and put his hands in his pockets.

"I'm sorry. I'm sorry. If you want me to leave, tell me.".

"I'm just trying to follow your lead here and you're confusing the hell out of me. Tell me what you want," he said quietly.

Juls rubbed her left arm where he had clasped it. She didn't know what she wanted. What the hell was she doing, she thought. It was those damned journals. They made her doubt everything.

"Jack, I need to get out of here, away from this for a while. This is swallowing me up whole. I thought I could get along through this, but I'm just confused."

"Where do you want to go? Do you want me to go with you or do you need time alone? Just tell me."

"Juls, I can do whatever you want," he continued.

She walked into her bedroom and sat down upon the bed, glancing around at her life there. It felt like an impostor's room, not hers. At this point, she felt she had lost all focus on everything, including who she was.

Across the room she saw the wedding photograph of her dad and mom on her dresser. She could use her dad's perspective right now and a walk on the beach in a place that seemed 10,000 miles away.

"Would you go to Florida with me? To my folks' house?" she asked, but before he could answer she answered for him.

"Of course, you can't. You have a life. What a stupid request. Sorry."

Jack knelt before her in the floor and took her hands, taking care not to squeeze her left hand.

"Give me a chance to answer, won't you?"

"Yes, I'll go. I said whatever you wanted, though I hadn't thought of going quite that far," he said and laughed.

She smiled at him and pushed his hair from his forehead.

"Can I afford it, the cost I mean?" she asked.

Jack laughed out loud. "My dear, you can afford it and much more. We just need to go by the bank on the way to the airport."

She looked up at the ceiling and laughed with him. Oh god, she did need this. And looking back at him, she realized that she needed him just as much and she smiled.

Chapter Seventeen

Summer 2010

Jack woke to the sound of the plane's wheels extending as the flight began its descent to the West Palm Beach airport where Juls's parents were probably already waiting for them.

Juls was a white knuckle flier and she had squeezed his arm through most of a fairly quiet flight.

Jack looked over to her face and saw that her eyes were squeezed shut. She may have been the worst flight companion he had ever had, but right now he wouldn't trade her company for anyone else's in the world.

She had called her parents before they left and told them they were flying down. Her dad was concerned with the suddenness of the visit. He knew she had been working with Jack about Julia's murder and he was afraid, not for any of the scandal touching him, but how it might affect Juls, especially if this guy were just using Juls for information about a book.

But her dad had not revealed any of this to either Juls or her mother. He would withhold his opinion until the appropriate time and talking on the phone did not sound like an opportune time to give her a warning. She had sounded fragile to him on the phone and he had never heard fragility in her voice before and it frightened him somewhat.

Elias Bell stood with his wife Katherine at the arrivals gate, barred by TSA rules from proceeding any further into the airport. Katherine had spent the morning preparing their spare bedrooms, shopping for food that would probably outlast Juls's visit, and generally fussing about their condo trying to find things to help pass the time before their arrival this evening.

Elias saw Juls first and then the tall, broad shouldered man following her carrying luggage for the both of them. He appeared nothing like Elias had thought he would. He looked like any ordinary tourist in a white polo and blue jeans. Nor did he look much older than Juls. But Elias was more careful to search for the subtle traces of how this "Jack" person was treating his only daughter. Elias would break the man before allowing him to hurt Juls.

As Juls and Jack walked through the arrivals area, she could see her father's tall head and white shock of hair above anyone else in the waiting her. She grabbed Jack's hand and led him quickly in their direction.

Her mother reached her first and embraced her as if the past two years had been a decade. Although she spoke with her mother almost every day, Juls did not realize how much she had missed her parents until standing there in the middle of the West Palm Beach Airport with them again.

Juls made all the appropriate introductions and Jack stood back a bit allowing them their moment of reunion before they left the airport for the parking building. The short distance between the terminal and the parking building allowed the blinding white Florida sunshine to overwhelm his senses for a moment. He had not forgotten his prescription sunglasses and pulled a pair of Wayfarers from his bag to protect his eyes.

While Katherine chattered away with Juls, Elias watched as Jack switched the glasses and saw what Juls had seen when the glasses were removed – the removal of his disguise. And that disturbed Elias a great deal. He knew too much about disguises from his own family. He had come to Florida to escape the Bells and their disguises, their pretense at normalcy, their deceit, and what he thought to be their theft of his great-grandmother's life.

Jack saw Elias's close perusal of him and offered a small smile in return. He saw in Elias the same hard protective shell that Juls kept around herself most of the time. What is it with these people, he asked himself, and then walked ahead of Elias to catch up with Juls and her mother.

Their accommodations at Juls's parents' condominium were exactly what he had expected – separate rooms, with him placed in what he always called the "fish" room, the nickname he gave to the worst guest room in anyone's home feeling that situations such as these were where the Benjamin Franklin saying about fish and guests usually applied.

Juls shrugged her shoulder subtly as if to say "sorry", but followed her mother to the larger guest room to begin unpacking the few things she had brought.

Jack had walked back into the living room and was staring at the ocean from the sliding doors of the Bells' third floor condo when Elias entered the room and came to stand next to him silently.

"Quite a view," Jack said trying to break the uncomfortable silence.

There weren't too many men who intimidated Jack, but then again, there weren't too many men who were as tall and as forceful with their presence as Elias Bell. He stood next to Jack more as a retired captain of industry rather than the geology professor he had spent his life as.

"Yes, it is," Elias said.

"Listen, I want to get this out before Juls comes back in here. I don't know you and I don't know what you want with my daughter or our family. I'm going to give you the benefit of the doubt simply for her, but," he paused and looked Jack in the eyes, "if your intent is to use her and toss her, you'll not find a worse enemy than me."

The color drained from Jack's face, but he did not break eye contact with Elias.

"How much has Juls told you?" Jack asked.

Elias turned his head back to the beach and the breaking waves.

"Not much. Not much. I just wanted to have my say before she came in."

Behind them, Juls and Katherine had heard the entire conversation. While Katherine was embarrassed by Elias's overprotective nature, she was not surprised by it. Elias had never been a politic man. It had kept him from being department chairman many times as younger men and women passed him by in their ascendancy to the position. Katherine squeezed Juls's hand and offered her a smile, but Juls did not seem in the least bit disturbed by her father's defense. For her, he had always been that way and she loved him for it whether she had liked it or not.

"Well, there's certainly no reason for anyone to be protecting me," Juls said and moved into the room, pulling her mother with her.

Both men turned to them and both appeared a bit red-faced at the conversation the two women had just overheard.

"Sit down, Dad. Jack and I need to talk to you and Mom before we do anything, including going to eat."

Juls moved to Jack's side and led him to the love seat to sit with her there. Elias went to Katherine and sat with her upon the pale yellow sofa facing Juls and Jack.

Juls began the story of the past week, even holding her hand up at one point to explain her wounded left arm. She told them of the hidden trunk, the journals, the money in the journals, and that they had just begun to go through the journals when she told them that she felt a bit overwhelmed by the whole experience. She watched as their faces went from being concerned to being confused to being shocked. She left out the parts about McKenzie Bell's sexual sadism, but she did paint as true a picture as possible of him as she could without the more torrid details.

Elias placed his hands together in front of his face and rested his chin on his thumbs for a moment. It was almost too much to take in. Katherine placed her hand at her husband's neck and began to softly stroke his back. She knew this was going to change his life and their lives and she feared what the disclosure of any of this might do to him.

"I can't believe that we never found the trunk before now," Elias said. "I grew up in that house. You grew up there. Your mother and I lived there together over 20 years. How could we not see the door or the trunk?"

He moved his hands from his mouth and then clenched them into fists. "How could my father not know about it?"

At this point, Katherine slid away from Elias and removed her hand from his back.

"I found the door and saw the trunk there years ago, but I never said anything about it," she said and looked down at the beige carpeting.

Elias stood suddenly, towering over her and said "What? You found it and you didn't tell me? Why the hell didn't you? Why would you keep it from me.?"

Katherine stood and faced him defiantly. "Exactly because of the way you're reacting now," she said and walked out of the room toward their bedroom.

Juls and Jack watched the entire conversation in surprise. Juls had never seen her father react so violently and it frightened her. This was the Bell side of him, she thought.

Jack leaned toward her and whispered that he thought he might walk down to the beach so she could talk with her parents. She nodded and as he left the condo. She saw that her father was still in the same position as when her mother had left the room – his hands clenched at his sides and his face flushed with anger.

"Dad, after what I found, after what I've read, I believe that she may have thought she was protecting you."

"From what?" he yelled. "From my family history? From my inheritance?"

Juls stood and went to his side and took one of his clenched fists in her right hand.

"No, not from that. From this," she said and lifted his fist upward.

Elias looked at his hand as if it were an alien appendage to his body. He relaxed his hand immediately and then his face flushed with color as he looked toward the direction his wife had taken.

"I would never hurt your mother. I have never . . . You know that. She must know that," he said.

"I know, Dad. I know. But there are things in our family history, maybe in our genetic make-up that even we cannot face. That's why Jack and I came down here. I couldn't stand to spend another moment in that house after reading many of those journals."

"I didn't know that she knew the trunk was there, but I would bet money that she had no idea what was in it. I think she was just trying to protect us," Juls said.

Elias started to walk toward his bedroom.

"I've got to make things right with your mother. Uh, can you and Jack . . ."

"Sure, Dad. We'll go grab some take-out and bring it back. Give you and Mom some time to talk. But Dad, there's one thing we never got to tell you and I need to tell you this before I go find Jack."

He turned back to her and waited.

"Ok. Tell me. I really need to talk to your mom."

She took a deep breath. Ok, here it goes, she thought.

"Dad we found almost 9 million dollars in the journals," she said.

"You found what?" His eyebrows raised as his voice lowered.

"Around 9 million dollars. Well, at least in collector's value. Around 5 million in face value."

He sat in the armchair next to the sofa.

"Oh my god," he said and held his head in his hands.

Chapter Eighteen

Summer 2010

Juls found Jack standing next to the pool at the ocean side of the condominium building. He was watching the last of the surfers paddling inland for the evening as the shadows of the building began to join the darkening distant horizon.

Past the building, the sunset glittered on the water in a few last spots and the warm sub-tropical wind blew a pleasant breeze inland on the patio.

Juls took Jack's hand in hers and stood quietly next to him, savoring the beauty of the early evening and the pull she always felt when standing near the ocean. But standing there with Jack she allowed herself to feel something different for the first time in her life. She couldn't quite name it. She just felt it - not alone.

"How's it going upstairs?" he said, pulling her closer and lightly kissing the top of her blonde head.

She sighed. Her mother had thrown them a real curve ball with her revelation and she hoped that it would not cause more problems for her parents or for them.

Leaning against Jack's shoulder, she placed her arm around his waist in response to his own arm encircling her waist.

"I honestly don't know. I feel like I've made their lives worse by trying to make mine easier to deal with," she said.

Jack turned to her and nodded his understanding to her fears. When he had had begun this "little" adventure with her, he would have tried to dismiss her fears, but after finding out so much about the Bell family, he found it impossible to offer her even the smallest bit of solace. The Bell family seemed hard and proud people who did not seem to forgive easily. He had wondered several times if he and Juls could remain friends after this. This was a family that buried secrets so deeply that they barely allowed themselves to have acquaintances, much less close friendships.

He looked out at the ocean again and saw an older man in a worn beach cap and headphones using a metal detector as he walked down the coast. Waving the detector back and forth in front of his bare feet like a dowsing rod, the man would stop every so often and pull something from the sand. Sometimes the man would pocket it and other times he would cast it back out toward the ocean.

Jack thought about Katherine and was worried for her. Elias seemed to be a cold man to him and Jack hoped that over 30 years of marriage would not be lost because Katherine had kept one secret from Elias.

He shook his head as if trying to shake the concerns for this family off and turned his attention to Juls.

"So, what's the plan?" he asked.

"I told Dad we'd go get some take-out and bring supper back to the condo. I don't think Mom is going to be feeling much like cooking tonight and I thought our absence might be good to give them some time to talk," she replied.

"I think they'll be ok. I'm just worried if they can find their way forward together. Learning about the secret she kept and then about the money . . . that's a lot to take in for him."

Jack brought her into his arms into a warm hug and leaned his head against the top of hers.

"It'll be ok. I don't know how, but it will," he said and led her away from the pool and toward the condo to go in search of food.

Neither of them had been aware that Elias and Katherine had been watching them from the balcony of their condo. Elias placed his arm around Katherine and hugged her in much the same way that Jack had hugged Juls.

"I think she's going to be ok," he said. Just as Jack had said to Juls, Elias wasn't sure why, but he felt it and for the first time in years he could feel as if the Bell curse was being lifted from them all.

Chapter Nineteen

Summer 2010

Juls and Jack returned with enough Mexican food for 10 people. When they had entered the restaurant they had not thought about just how hungry they were and without knowing what to get her parents, they had made a wide selection of the offerings on the menu.

They arrived back at the condo to find Elias and Katherine setting the table together and they could hear them laughing as Juls opened the door. She smiled up at

Jack and felt reassured for the first time since her revelations to her parents.

Jack had stopped at a liquor store along the way and had bought a bottle of tequila and a bottle of Argentinean Conches E Toro wine. He had asked Juls if they drank at all and she said yes and that his choices were good and considering the circumstances of the late afternoon's event, probably a good idea as well.

As they entered the condo, Elias moved to help Jack with the bags of food as Juls began helping her mother pull serving dishes from the cabinets in the small galley kitchen. While Elias and Jack worked from one side of an open bar, the women put the steaming food onto platters and into bowls which Jack then carried to the table.

Elias held up the bottles and looked to the three of them.

"What say we start with the wine and move to the Tequila after supper?" They all laughed and moved to the table and spent the next hours talking with one another over the good food and delicious wine.

Jack had noticed that any mention of the trunk or money was carefully kept tucked away. He had spent part of the evening relating his travels in researching his books and he and Elias were surprised to find that they had visited many of the same places.

"I remember taking Katherine and Juls to Indonesia on one of my first research trips after Juls was born. It was a beautiful place, but Juls was terrified of the dragons," Elias said.

Juls lifted her head and looked at her father in shock.

"When was this?" she asked.

"Oh, you were about three or four years old, so it must have been sometime in the mid to late 80s," he said as he sipped his wine.

"Dad, are you serious? I have really been to the Indonesia? I really saw Komodo Dragons there?"

Katherine stood and began clearing the table. She remembered those horrible lizards.

"Of course, he's sure, Juls. I didn't like them anymore than you did, actually. Vile and dangerous and huge. I remember wanting to get back to the boat as fast as possible when I saw them. You and I were running back to the boat and you screamed the entire time. I was afraid we had traumatized you forever, but once we were back on the research ship it was as if we were never there," she said.

"No wonder I have the nightmares," Juls said.

Elias put his glass on the table and looked at Juls and asked, "What nightmares?"

"I've been having nightmares about being chased by Komodo Dragons for the past month. I thought maybe it had something to do with something I saw on the Discovery Channel."

"Wow. It wasn't a nightmare. It was a real memory," she said. Her hand shook slightly and she drained the full contents of her wine glass in one quick drink.

Jack watched them in amazement. This was the weirdest family. Didn't they ever talk to one another, he wondered. And talk about repressed memories. This one was a real doozy if Juls was having nightmares about it now.

"I'm making Margaritas if anyone's interested," Katherine said from the kitchen.

Jack said that he was and jumped up to help with clearing the last of the dishes from the table as Katherine ran the blender and mixed the drinks.

By the time they were settled down in the living room with their drinks in much the same position that they had sat when Juls had first told them about the trunk, they all could feel what was coming, but this time, with the help of full bellies and the tequila, they didn't feel as hesitant about talking.

Jack was quiet through most of the evening, observing their interactions and listening to their theories about what had really happened to Julia Bell in 1937.

At one point, Katherine saw the difference the money was about to make for the three of them.

"My god, the money." She looked to Elias and asked, "Does this mean I can stop worrying about the damn electric bill?"

They all laughed at that.

"Yes, my dear. I think we can safely pay our electric bill on time now without worrying about buying groceries," Elias said. "

Juls can even get out of that mini-mausoleum and find something she likes, not something she was sort of dropped into," he said.

"Hey," Juls said. "I like my mini-mausoleum. And don't call it that. I've made it my own home. If you'd bothered to visit in the last two years, you'd know that."

Elias laughed. "Sorry, Juls, I know you love the house, but I never did. Too many bad things about growing up there, I suppose."

"But, Dad, you and Mom made it a wonderful home for me. I never had those bad memories. Think about what we shared there, what you and Mom shared there. It was good. It was."

Katherine stood and took Elias's hand.

"She's absolutely right, Elias. It wasn't just good. It was wonderful," she said and smiled.

Elias looked from Juls to his wife. "I guess it was, wasn't it?" and he stood next to his wife.

"Good night you two," Katherine said. "If you need anything, let me know. But my tired knees are telling me it's bedtime."

After Elias and Katherine retired to their bedroom, Juls and Jack sat quietly with one another on the love seat. She leaned her cheek against the thick cotton knit of his polo shirt covering his shoulder.

"I guess we should call it a night, too," he said and lifted her mouth to his and kissed her good-night.

"I'll see you in the morning."

Juls took his hand and stopped him as he started to head towards the fish room.

"Wait, I'm coming with you," she said.

He paused and then looked at her. He did so want to sleep with her tonight, but he knew he couldn't.

"Juls, I'd love that more than you could know, but I can't do it. Your folks made two rooms for us for a reason and I won't disrespect that," he said.

She sighed and agreed he was right, but followed him to his bedroom door and kissed him deeply and longingly.

"That's what you're missing tonight," she said.

He groaned a bit. "Oh, please don't remind me," he said as she closed the door between them and headed to her own bed.

Chapter Twenty

Summer 2010

Juls walked the beach with her father early the next morning before the tourists hit the shore and staked their claims with their beach umbrellas and surf boards and towels. The water was warm on her bare feet as the low tide lapped in small wavelets on the hard packed sand.

"So, are you serious about this guy, Juls?"

She shrugged. She liked him so much, but she had never learned to trust and that was an obstacle she would have to overcome first.

"I like him, if it makes any difference. So does your mom. We've watched him with you, how he does things for you, how he seems to put you first," Elias said looking forward without facing Juls.

"And especially that he respected the two bedroom line," he added.

Juls blushed. TMI, her friend Bobbie would have said. Too much information. All Juls could do was bob her head.

"I can't say what will happen once we go back to Huntington and start going through the journals again. I haven't reacted very well to reading them," she said.

Elias stopped and picked up a small shell fragment and skipped it across the placid low tide.

"Then don't read them. Take the money out and toss them. Burn them. They're yours to do with as you wish, though Jack is right about the money. I don't know of any other family members still living, but we need to do this legally, even if it means sharing the money with some long lost cousin," he said.

Juls stopped on the beach and watched the sun growing smaller as it rose above the horizon.

"No, I'm going to read them for Julia's sake. Dad, she was tortured by her husband. Someone needs to bear witness to her suffering. Someone needs to know what her life became. Besides we may find something in those journals that could lead us to what happened to her."

"Well, whatever you want to do is fine. They're yours. I don't want to know, though. I don't want to think that my grandfather was as horrible as his father. I've spent my life trying to escape what I've always called "the Bell curse." Except for the money, I'm done with it all," he said.

She nodded her acknowledgement of his feelings and began to walk with him again. Now that the sun was rising, the early sunbathers were starting to appear here and there and they both turned to head back to the condo.

Katherine and Jack were in the midst of cooking a huge breakfast when they arrived home. Elias walked over to his wife and kissed her lightly.

"Damn, that smells good," he said.

She laughed. "Thank Jack. He's done most of the work. I've just mostly directed him towards ingredients."

The four of them spent the rest of the week enjoying the Florida sunshine. Juls and her mother went shopping over at the Sawgrass Mills Mall and Jack and Elias even found time to play a couple rounds of golf at the Sawgrass course while they shopped.

Elias said he had always wanted to join the Sawgrass, but never could see putting the money into something that he and Katherine couldn't really afford. But now, well, he said he guessed he could afford it.

Juls and her parents had spent their lives being frugal and while they weren't being extravagant, they were indulging themselves with a few things that had been unattainable before finding Julia's money. Elias had not only bought himself the membership to Sawgrass, he had also bought himself a new set of Calloway Clubs, golf clothes and had offered to buy the same for Jack. But Jack demurred, and used a set of guest clubs, saying to Elias that he didn't play often enough to justify Elias spending the money. He also did not want to feel indebted to Elias. He didn't want Elias to think that his interest in Juls was merely mercenary.

If Juls were rich, she would be rich and her money would be hers. Always. He cared too much about her to ever have her think that he had taken advantage of her in any way. He made enough money to support himself and to travel. His books sold quite well so he did not worry excessively about money, but he also had few wants other than the equipment he needed to do his job and the money to pay for him to travel when necessary. Beyond the basics of food, shelter and clothing, he had more than he needed.

And, as he told Elias, he knew he did not need a new set of Calloway Clubs. As he spent more time with Elias, the more he came to admire him. Elias was an extraordinary man who held firmly to his scruples and code of ethics, even when it cost him advancement in his field. Elias was also a first class scientist and Jack believed that Marshall University had been lucky to have a scientist such as him on their staff. He thought about Katherine's remark about being able to pay the electric bill and he winced inwardly. Somehow that just didn't seem right to him - a man of Elias's intelligence and talent relegated to retirement hell in which only educators seem to be stuck.

Juls, on the other hand, was indulging her mother. She knew that there were so many things that her mother would have loved to have been able to have but could never afford. She took her shopping at the Sawgrass mall first and then decided to drive them down to the Doral and spent the entire day being pampered in the Doral's first class spa.

Juls actually wanted to buy them whatever they wanted, but she also knew that the money belonged to all of them and that if her parents did want something, they would get it. She supposed in the end that she just wanted to spend the week with them and be happy without worrying about work or school or money for the first time in their lives.

So, when Elias and Jack returned in the afternoons from either playing golf or deep sea fishing, they returned to find Juls and her mother giggling like school girls over clothing and spa treatments and what Katherine called "silly girl stuff." Most nights the four of them would dress and go out to dinner and enjoy long, gourmet meals and fine wine. And each night Jack found himself wishing more and more he hadn't turned Juls away from his door that first night. It was as if she glowed that week. She smiled and laughed all the time and he saw that the happiness broke the shell away from her, allowing herself for the first time in her life to lower her guard.

The week went by far too fast for all of them. Elias had truly come to like Jack and both he and Katherine strongly believed that Jack and Juls loved one another whether they had discovered it yet or not. He fretted a bit about them going back to Huntington. He was afraid that the Bell curse would be waiting there to ruin their chances at finding happiness with one another.

He knew this from experience as he and Katherine had spent three interminable years fighting before they simply gave up and loved one another unreservedly. She had no idea, but sometimes when she was doing the most mundane household chore, he would look at her and think about how lucky he had been to have found her and his love would be as strong as it had been 30 years ago.

Elias and Katherine watched as Juls and Jack passed through the gates to the boarding area having made promises to call when they arrived and to keep them informed of their progress on the legal aspects of the inheritance they had found in Julia's trunk. They waved good-bye until both Juls and Jack disappeared from view and then headed back home. And for the first time in years, they both felt so alone, missing the vibrant presence of their daughter and Jack.

Katherine took Elias's hand as they walked away.

"Don't worry. They're going to be happy and they're going to be ok," she said smiling.

He placed his arm around her shoulder and hugged her tightly. He hoped to god that she was right.

Chapter Twenty-One

Summer 2010

The house was musty and smelled bad when they opened the front door upon their return. They walked through the house and could track the smell emanating from the dining room. The old trunk and the journals, locked in a hot small house in warm weather, had created a miasma of odors, none of which was pleasant.

Juls took a look into the dining room and then walked past it to take her bags into her bedroom. Jack had left his bag in the rental car. He hadn't decided whether staying here was a wise decision. He had followed Juls from the car to the house carrying her bags and she had not noticed that his bag was not with the others.

She went to the spare room to look for him and was surprised not to see him there. She called his name and was relieved when she heard him return her call from the front of the house. She found him standing in front of her collection of first editions in much the same place he had stood so many weeks ago.

"What are you doing?" she asked.

Jack pushed his hands deep in his pockets to keep himself from touching her. And god, after the past week, he really wanted to touch her, kiss her, and carry her to that back bedroom and make love to her.

"I can't stay here, Juls. Not right now. There's a lot of work to do if you decide to keep the journals or if you decide to let me read them. Either way, my staying here complicates everything."

She was not happy. She crossed her arms and stood in front of him, almost challenging him not to come closer.

"I don't see how your staying here could possibly complicate anything. Unless, you have ulterior motives, which you swore to me you did not. So tell me the real reason you want to leave. Don't give me any line of bullshit about "complications."

Jack stepped back from her and hit his shin against the sharp corner of a low Stickley table. He grimaced and turned to step behind the table.

"That is the truth," he said. "How can we be lovers and work on this together? The last time we tried you pushed me away. I don't want that. I don't know what I want, but I don't want that."

He bowed his head and then looked out the large front window of the living room. The mid afternoon sunshine gave a different color to the world than the hot Florida sunshine had. Bright yellows and greens replaced the bright whites and blues he had gotten used to over the past week.

"Yes, I was very stressed before we left. You have to admit I had good reason to be. But it had nothing to do with you. In fact, you've been the one who's gotten me through this. Why do you always want to leave?" she asked.

"Is it something that happened before Florida? You've barely touched me since that morning we left. Is it . . . Oh, hell, forget it. Just go ahead and go. I'm smart enough to get all this done. Just leave. I'm tired of asking you to be with me. I'm not so dense that I can't figure out that you don't want to be with me."

She turned to walk away and he took her hand. For him, it was all he needed to give him a reason to stay. But she was angry and hurt and he had to find a way to make things right between them.

"Juls, I've wanted to be with you since we left, but I didn't want you to look at me ever again the way you did the morning after you read the first journals. That was really hard. I felt as if you hated me and every man you'd ever known. I don't want that."

His knee was really throbbing now.

She moved toward him and hit her knee on the same corner of the Stickley table. "Damn it," she said and sat down to rub her leg.

Jack sat down on the Stickley sofa next to her and leaned his head back against the leather cushions.

"I don't want you to ask me to stay and then regret it," he said.

"The only thing I'm regretting right now is buying this damn table," she said and continued to rub her knee.

Jack wanted to laugh, but his shin was hurting as much as her knee.

"Well, we're not bleeding," he said and then she looked up at him and began to laugh, falling back against his chest.

"I'll stay if you want," he said and hugged her to his chest. "And only if we can put this damn table somewhere out of the way."

She smiled and nodded, trying not to let him see that she was close to tears. She was afraid that he found her unappealing. The words from Julia's journals that McKenzie had repeatedly said when he raped her came back to Juls's mind.

"You're ugly. You're homely. You're a cow. I can't stand looking at your face," he had said to Julia as he raped her.

Being Julia's great-great granddaughter, she was afraid that Jack had found her equally repulsive. Pushing her away in Florida and now just having said he wanted to leave had made her feel horrible. She could only imagine how McKenzie's words had made Julia feel then, if over 135 years later they made her feel ugly.

Jack stood and carefully led her around the table through the house, past the dining room and toward the bedroom they had shared that wonderful afternoon and evening together. As he sat her upon the bed and knelt before her and began to unbutton her blouse, he saw that she had been about to cry. He gently kissed each eyelid and moved his mouth to hers, her mouth sweet and soft under the pressure of his lips.

She returned his kiss with equal ardor, removed his glasses, and held his face between his hands, then lay back and pulled him on top of her. She could feel him harden as his legs moved onto hers. She unzipped his jeans and freed him from the tight jockeys he wore beneath the jeans, stroking him slowly up and down. He closed his eyes for a moment as he held his weight above her.

"You're going to have to stop that for a moment or we're going to have a mess," he said and smiled.

She laughed and scrambled out from under him, removing her own clothing as quickly as she possibly could. By the time they were both undressed, he climbed atop her and as he entered her, he began to gently tug at her breasts with his teeth. She moaned and grasped his buttocks, pushing him harder into her and moving faster and faster with him. She could feel the heat of their bodies building together and their strong lovemaking shook the bed hard enough for the nightstand next to it to shake.

Neither of them noticed that the pictures frames fell to the floor. She lifted herself to his body, matching his movements equally, gasping as she could feel her passion for him building and peaking with his own.

When she felt as if the room had stopped turning, she clasped him tighter once more and felt a second set of tremors pass through her body. It was wonderful and almost as gratifying as the first. He lifted himself from her and leaned his weight on one arm. With his other hand he brushed her hair away from her face and smiled down at her.

"I hope you believe me now, Juls. That's about the best I can do to show you how I feel. You should know me well enough to know that I wouldn't have made love to you again if I didn't want to be with you," he said.

She rolled with him to lie on their sides, face to face. He looked so different without those hideous dark glasses. He was a beautiful man, far more handsome than she would ever be. She ran her fingers through his thick, dark hair and wondered if she allowed herself to love him if she would spend the rest of her life afraid that she would never compare to the women who would see beyond his disguise, much less the women who had come before her.

"You scare me," she said. "And you make me feel like no one else ever has." As she laid her hand upon his cheek, she explained her fears to him, the notions of her possible inadequacies brought about by the journals and his own experiences and her lack of experience.

"Juls, first, the journals have nothing to do with what goes on between us as far as intimacy is concerned. As to experience, well, hell, my dear, you have no worries in making me, uh, well, satisfied," he replied.

He sat up and looked down at her lying next to him on the bed. He had no idea where she had gotten the idea that she was less than beautiful and that was when he realized that he was falling in love with her. He could feel himself sinking down and good god, she was taking him to a place within himself he hadn't felt in a very, very long time.

Chapter Twenty-Two

Diary of Julia Chafin Bell
November 1879

My labor pains began this morning. I was sitting in the solarium of this mausoleum in which McKenzie has entombed me using my dowry money when I felt my skirts wet as if I had spilled a pitcher of warm water on my lap. I struggled to stand, but the first pain overwhelmed me and almost caused me to fall down. It seemed to take forever for me to reach the main house and call for Effie and it seemed to take almost as long for her to reach me. By the time I had her send her boy for Doctor Laidley and have her manage to get me to my bedroom and into my night gown, I was drenched with perspiration.

The pains were fairly steady and grew closer in rhythm. I began to fear that the doctor would not arrive in time and that Effie would be forced to deliver the baby alone. I wanted my mother there, but McKenzie had already forbidden her attendance at my bedside. For three years he had kept me as isolated as possible from my family, including my cousins who had become quite wealthy themselves with the sale of their land to Mr. Huntington.

But McKenzie was not here now and I was not going to allow him to dictate to me what I could and could not do right now. I grabbed Effie's hand and instructed her to find one of the grooms and send him with a carriage to bring my mother to me immediately.

She argued with me, telling me that Mr. Bell had instructed her to contact him first and not to have my family brought here when the child was ready to be born.

I grabbed her bodice front and said that if she did not bring my mother to me immediately that she would have much more to fear than Mr. Bell's displeasure. I do not believe she took my threat seriously, but I do believe she understood as a woman my need for my mother to be at my side and so she agreed and ran down to the stable to have my mother brought to me.

When she returned, she asked if she should send her son for Mr. Bell when the boy returned with the doctor. I was between pains and was breathing heavily, but I managed to tell her no. I did not need to tell her where McKenzie was. She knew as did most of the household servants and possibly most of Huntington society. He was over on Second Avenue with one of his whores. I thought to myself, let him stay there and come home later to discover whether or not his child had been born or whether his wife or child had managed to survive.

I hated him at that moment more than I ever had and I swore that if he tried to hurt me again that I would fight him with everything I had. I no longer believed that this was what God had intended for me as a wife. Only the Devil could create such pain and torture and I believed that McKenzie would be meeting the Devil himself one day. Until then, McKenzie was never going to hurt me again.

By the time the doctor had arrived, my mother appeared shortly thereafter and sat to the other side of my bed, holding my hand and wiping my forehead with a cold compress. Her soothing words and presence did not lessen the pain, but it did make it more bearable.

It was not too long after their arrival that the doctor laid upon my bedclothes a red, squalling infant who resembled his father. But it did not matter to me, I took the child into my arms after my mother and Effie had cleaned him and knew that I finally had someone in this world who would love me as much as I loved him.

Doctor Laidley asked if we had chosen a name for him so he could complete the birth certificate for us. McKenzie had wanted to name the baby after himself, but he was not here and so I named my beautiful son, Jeremiah, after my grandfather, only adding McKenzie as his second name because I knew McKenzie's wrath would be tremendous because I had not honored his wishes.

My mother stayed after the doctor left and asked if I wished to send Effie's boy for McKenzie. I blushed at the knowledge that even she knew where my husband could most likely be found. I told her no and she did not comment or ask again, but instead sat next to me and while marveling at the beauty of her newest grandchild, told me of all the latest news of my family. My cousins Robert and William had both sold much of their land, including the family landing to Mr. Huntington and that they had removed themselves to large homes they had built down the street from my own home.

She told me that now that my lying-in was over, I would be amazed by the changes in Huntington around where I now lived. She told me that the whole of that section of Third Avenue where I lived was now called "Millionaire's Row" and that almost every one of the families who had owned land above the Guyandotte River had prospered enormously. She related to me that even my brother, Christopher, had taken work with Mr. Huntington's railroad and was often away on business and rarely at home any more.

As darkness began to creep into the skies outside my bedroom window, my mother asked if I wished her to stay, but I told her "No" and that it would probably be best if she left before it got any later.

She smiled in understanding, bent and kissed me and my young Jeremiah and promised to returned as soon as I felt well enough to receive her again, gently couching her words in such a way that I knew that she meant she would return again as soon as McKenzie allowed her to do so.

It was after midnight when I heard McKenzie come into the house, slamming the front door without a care as to whether he might disturb anyone else. Effie had sat up next to the door and waited for his return to tell him of the day's events. As I lie in the bed holding my son closely to me, I placed a letter opener from my night table under my pillow in case I needed to protect myself or my child from McKenzie's anger.

When he burst into the room, he first looked over to the empty cradle and then to me. I expected him to curse me, but he did not. He approached me slowly and looked down at me and our child. He was beaming. He had produced a son and stood like a stupid cock about to bounce around a barnyard. He started to reach for Jeremiah, but I held fast and told him that the child was sleeping and the doctor said he could not be disturbed.

McKenzie stepped back and acquiesced without questioning my lie. It was then that he looked down and saw the birth certificate lying upon the nightstand. He waved it in the air and asked what it was and why his child was named Jeremiah. His face flushed bright red with anger and he raised his hand to slap me but stopped himself probably because at that moment the infant started to cry loudly.

So instead of hitting me, he balled up the birth certificate and threw it at me.

"I know why you did this. Well, it won't do any good. I'll have the certificate corrected first thing tomorrow. He is my son and he will carry my name," he said.

I returned his glare unafraid this time, a look he had never seen on my face before this moment.

"You will not," I said quietly, but firmly. "His name is Jeremiah. I do not think you want to embarrass yourself in front of the Laidleys, so you will leave things as they are.

He leaned across the bed putting his face as close to mine as possible. I could smell the whiskey and cigar smoke on his hot breath.

"Be careful, little girl or you will be punished. Not tonight or this week, but soon. Your defiance has doomed you," he hissed. He began to lose his balance and became unsteady positioned above me. He had to stand in order to regain his balance.

I wanted to plunge the letter opener into his heart at that moment, but I refrained because I knew Jeremiah needed me more that I needed McKenzie dead. So instead of continuing the argument, I simply smiled up at him. I was taking control of my life as much as I possibly could.

I opened my nightgown to offer my breast to Jeremiah while McKenzie stood over us and watched silently. As long as I had Jeremiah, I knew I had the strength to fight him. My son would make me strong, if nothing else could.

Chapter Twenty-Three

Diary of Julia Chafin Bell
February 1880

It has been a peaceful three months since Jeremiah's birth. I waited each night for McKenzie to collect upon his threat, but he seemed to have changed after the night of our son's birth. He did not return to my bedroom nor did he spend his evenings with his whores except for the occasional week night which he explained to me that he would be working late.

I did not care as long as he took his perversions elsewhere. He even made attempts to reconcile with my parents and invited them to dine with us on several occasions. The holidays were a happier time for me though I was still wary of him although he bought gifts for me, Jeremiah and my parents, pretending that the money he used was his own earnings and not my great dowry he had claimed from my father.

I should have been more careful and more aware of his predatory nature, but the reconciliation with my parents and the thriving young son I had distracted me just enough. When his punishment finally arrived, I was in no way prepared for it.

At the end of January, I fell ill with the grippe and Doctor Laidley advised McKenzie to remove Jeremiah from the house to protect him. McKenzie was so gracious about taking our son to my parents and was so solicitous of my health that I simply forgot the Devil lived within him.

After a week had passed, my fever broke. When I finally awoke from my delirium, I found that he had sent the servants away as well and that I was left alone with him. Effie would cook at home and bring food to the back door where she left it as instructed by McKenzie. She later told me that he seemed "most concerned" for her and her son's well being and that he had said that he would care for me himself.

If only I had known. If only.

The second night after I had begun feeling better, I got up from my sickbed and went in search of him as I heard no answers from him to my calls. I was halfway down the staircase when he entered from the rear of the house, staggering somewhat as he spied me on the steps. I turned to ascend the staircase back to my bedroom when he called my name out. I froze when I heard the drunken tenor of his voice and I knew that I was in trouble.

"Behold the whore of my home," McKenzie said loudly.

I ran up the rest of the stairs and into my bedroom, locking the door and looking for some method of escape from the house, but even the simple exertion of running up the steps left me breathless. As I could hear his heavy body slamming against the door, I ran to a corner of the room and cowered in the floor and began to pray for some rescue from whatever McKenzie had planned for me.

I wish I could say that my memories of that night are blurred by the pain and shame of what happened, but in reality I know every detail, as he savagely raped me that night.

Later, McKenzie sat at my dressing table, drinking and smoking as he enjoyed my humiliation as much as he had enjoyed my muffled screams of pain. At one point during the ordeal, as I had been nursing my baby, my milk let down and he drunkenly laughed and said, "Keep that disgusting liquid for our son, I'd rather have a piece of your tail."

After a while I thought he had begun to tire and that the drink was starting to dull his senses, but I was again mistaken. McKenzie grabbed my legs and I tried to scramble away from him as I knew what he had planned for my final humiliation of the evening.

I lost track of time at some point after that and mercifully, by the time I saw the light in the eastern sky, I had passed out from the pain. When I woke up a few hours later, I found myself alone and untied. I crawled from the bed and tried to find my wash stand with eyes that were almost swollen shut from being beaten and having wept so much.

McKenzie returned to my room several hours later and stood over my bed.

"If you ever defy me again, the punishment will be far more severe. By law you are my property to do with as I wish and that is exactly what you will do. You will obey me completely or find yourself being punished again."

As he started to leave the room, he stopped and offered one last warning, "And if you say a word about this to anyone, you will be taken to the state mental facility where I will have you committed permanently, thanks to a little known state law that a friendly doctor here in town told me about after having to have a local woman taken there for her dipsomania."

I have not stopped weeping since he left this morning. I am doomed. My life is over.

Chapter Twenty-Four

Summer 2010

Jack was disgusted by what he had just read in the journal. Julia had turned over the reading to him as she felt she couldn't bear the pain of reading it anymore. All their plans to carefully conserve the journals and take care of them seemed to be a useless endeavor now to both of them. He wouldn't want this information known about his family and he could certainly understand why Juls wanted as little to do with it as possible.

She returned to work the week after they had returned from Florida and left him to take care of the "journal problem." Since he had brought this horror down upon her, he was determined to see it through to the end, but reading entries such as the one he had just finished was making it difficult for even him. He knew that Juls could not read this particular journal.

He closed the books up and placed the ones he had completed in one of the empty archival boxes. The rest he moved into the trunk and shoved it into a far corner of the dining room. He saw no need to have any of it lying about as a reminder to Juls of what horrors the books might hold for her.

Jack walked into the kitchen to pour a cup of coffee and happened to look up at the calendar on the wall next to Juls's refrigerator. He had been here over a month since their excursion to Florida. Their relationship had grown comfortable and felt right for him, but he was feeling restless with what he now saw as an endeavor that held no future for any book he might want to write.

He had tried unsuccessfully to return to the book on Collis Huntington several times, but could never remove from his mind the presence of McKenzie Bell in Collis

Huntington's plans for the city. Disgust was the best word for him to use in describing Bell and Bell had trapped him here as surely as he had trapped Julia in that house on early Huntington's "millionaire's row."

There were times in which Jack would actually be angrier with Julia Chafin Bell than her pig of a husband and then he would force himself to remember that she was a child of her time, a time when god and obedience to one's husband was first in the life of any well brought up young woman. Sex was never discussed except by women of low standards and Julia would never have associated with women of that sort.

When Juls came through the door that evening, she greeted him with a kiss and quick embrace, before carrying her briefcase and purse into her bedroom. Jack sat down upon the Stickley sofa and waited for her to return.

Juls saw his restlessness, but pretended that it was not there. She was so sure that he was going to greet her one evening with the news that he was leaving on another assignment that some days she dreaded the short drive from her office to her home. She knew he had no real reason to stay anymore, but thinking of his absence made her chest hurt.

So she was unsurprised by his statement to her as she returned to the living room. To say that she had seen it coming would be an understatement, but she had hoped to have just a little more time with him.

"Juls, I'm not getting anywhere with those journals, I don't see any answers there and, well, she couldn't very well have ended the last one by writing who her murderer was unless she wrote a final entry as a ghost," he said when she came and sat next to him.

She nodded. She knew that. She had hired a local lawyer to do what was necessary regarding Julia's money and finding out if Julia had had other descendants so that, too, was a job for which Jack's skills weren't necessary,

Jack took her left hand in his and looked at the angry red scar that was all that remained to remind him of what they had been trying to discover.

"At least we found the money for you and your parents. None of you needs to worry about money again. That should provide some solace," he said.

"I am at a dead end with the Huntington book and I certainly can't write about Jonas now or your family. I need to be working. Sitting here in this house, reading those journals is starting to depress even me."

Juls knew he was telling her he was leaving and this time she would accept it gracefully, rather than shutting him out or throwing a tantrum.

She would be an adult. She loved him and she felt that he loved her, but she also knew that Huntington was not enough for him, that he would always want to find a new book to work on in some foreign place that would take him very far away from her.

Watching him walk away was going to be the hardest thing she had ever done, but she was going to do it. For him. He might come back, she thought, but in her heart she didn't think he would.

"It's ok, Jack. Really. I've been lucky to have you help me this much. You're absolutely right about the things that are left to do can be handled by our lawyer. I'm not being fair to you asking you to do what I won't even try to do," she said and stood up in front of him.

He took her hands with his and pulled her closer to his body.

"Juls, I don't want to leave you. I want to stay with you. I'd even stay here in Huntington with you, but I can't just sit around all day not working. I need to work as much as I need you."

She lowered her head to hide the tears forming in the corners of her eyes, but then lifted her head and tried to give him her brightest smile.

"So how long do we have before you leave?" she asked. "A day, a few days? Do you have another project lined up yet?"

He stood and held her close, leaning her head against his shoulder. "I don't have anything lined up, but I thought I'd start doing some looking so we have some time before we know where I'll be going and for how long."

"For how long you'll be gone? Aren't you leaving for good?" she asked, puzzled at his response.

He laughed and hugged her tightly.

"Juls, I'm not leaving you. I just need to find a book project. I'll be back. I promise. Hell, you can even go with me if you want. You don't have to work editing other people's copy all day anymore. You can do whatever you want now," he said.

She hadn't thought of it in those terms. She didn't have to work anymore. She could do what ever she wanted now, even start her own business if she wanted or write a book herself. Julia Chafin Bell's money had made that possible.

"I don't know, Jack. I don't know what I want to do, except be with you."

"I know, Juls. I feel the same way. I've fallen in love with you, crazy ancestors and all. The only thing I know besides the fact that I need you now is that fact that I also know I need to get back to work," he said.

"Then we'll figure something out," she said, "Because I love you, too. Ugly glasses and all," she finished and they both laughed together loudly.

Chapter Twenty-Five

The Diary of Julia Chafin Bell
June 1891

I had crawled under an iron bed in one of the unused servant's rooms with Jeremiah. It was so hot in the house that my clothing was dripping wet. I could not ever remember being so hot in all my life and the Ohio River Valley had always been hot and humid. I hugged Jeremiah close to my body. At least his fever had finally broken. I thanked God for that great blessing. The fever had wracked his body for days. Doctor Laidley had diagnosed him with typhus and had temporarily quarantined the house although he had told both McKenzie and me that typhus was rampant in the city from the recent flood.

"Always is after a flood. We warn people to stay out of the water and not to drink it for a few weeks after the floods, but people ignore it. One of the few times that the Temperance Society creates more problems than it solves," he had told us.

I had listened little to what he had had to say after that, trying to focus all my attention on taking care of Jeremiah.

The doctor had left a tincture which he said should help with any pain that Jeremiah might suffer, but that only time and the good Lord could do anything now.

I had pushed both men from Jeremiah's room, unafraid of anything that McKenzie would say or do to me this time. I had held Jeremiah's small hand in mine, wiping his forehead with cool cloths and giving him sips of honey lemon tea laced with a little of McKenzie's bourbon. It was a home recipe my grandmother had given me when I had been ill as a child and it had always soothed my throat and chest.

But I saw that this was a much different disease than anything I had ever had as a child. All I could do was minister to Jeremiah's basic needs and pray as I listened to each of his breaths.

Effie had tried to help me and even McKenzie had astounded me by offering to sit with Jeremiah so I could rest, but I had refused and I fiercely ordered him from my son's bedroom.

The hours had passed so slowly and Jeremiah had remained unconscious for most of the time. Finally, McKenzie had forced his way into the room, past the high boy I had barricaded the door with and entered to find me holding Jeremiah tight to my chest.

"Julia, you must let us take care of him now and you must rest," he said quietly.

I had heard that quiet tone in McKenzie's voice before and this time I believed that he meant to punish me for disobeying him earlier, possibly by removing Jeremiah from my care. I would not allow it. No one could care for him better than I could.

As McKenzie left the room, I could hear him running down the front staircase and I had wrapped Jeremiah in a silk quilt and had stolen away down the hall towards the servants' wing of the house, finding one of the empty housemaids' rooms and had softly closed the door, locked it and then had crawled under the bed, dragging Jeremiah with me on the quilt and pulling his cooler body to me.

I could hear McKenzie and Effie going through the main house, calling my name. I wanted to curse Effie for helping McKenzie, but I was aware that Effie had no choice when McKenzie ordered her to do something. After the birth of Jeremiah and Effie's failure to send someone to find McKenzie, he had done something to Effie that had changed her. I never discovered what it was, but I knew from that time onward that Effie was more afraid of McKenzie than I was.

I also knew that if McKenzie found us he would kill me this time without hesitation. He had never forgiven me for failing to name Jeremiah after him and for the past 10 years he had punished me on more than one occasion, sometimes just beating me when the whiskey had caused him to lose his manhood.

I was thankful for one thing – McKenzie had never lain a hand upon Jeremiah. He loved the child as if love were something of which he was actually capable. He did not care that Jeremiah looked like my family and did not resemble his father except in expressions. Oh, McKenzie, without his sexual sickness and his weakness for drink, could be a good man in the eyes of Huntington society. Very few people knew the type of man he truly was,

But I knew I could not let him take Jeremiah from me. I knew if he did, he would take Jeremiah off to New York or Chicago and stay there and not allow me to ever see my son again and I knew that I could not live if that were to happen.

I pulled Jeremiah closer to my body and stroked his head and whispered, "It's going to be okay. Mother will not let anything happen. I will protect you," and I kissed his head and snuggled closer to him despite the heat in the closed room that made me almost faint. It was only my desperation to protect him that kept me from passing out. My fear of McKenzie was so great that I shivered so much that I could feel my body shaking against Jeremiah under the quilt.

Again, it seemed as if hours passed as I listened for McKenzie and now other strange voices calling my name. I remembered his threat of having me committed to an asylum and I began to sob. Oh God, please help me. Do not let him find us.

But my prayers failed as I heard the door knob shaking and a voice calling to my husband. They had found us. I heard a key opening the door and saw McKenzie's feet from beneath the bed.

"Julia, for god's sake, what are you doing?" he said and grabbed under the bed for my arm. I crawled away from him and I could hear him directing others to help him get me and Jeremiah from under the bed. I fought them as hard as I could, but it was impossible. Their strength was too great and I was so weak after nursing Jeremiah. I screamed and wailed as they pulled me away from my son.

To my surprise, Dr. Laidley was among them and he advanced towards me and held my face, forcing my mouth open as others' arms held mine.

I did not expect him to assist McKenzie in this endeavor. He had always seemed a good and kind man and now I realized that I was lost, but at the time I had no idea how lost I truly was.

"She's infected, as well," the doctor said. "Take her to her room and put her in bed. I'll be there shortly."

I began to struggle and scream, "No, no, leave my son alone. I'm fine."

McKenzie advanced toward me as I watched them remove Jeremiah from under the bed, his body still wrapped in the silk quilt.

I spat at McKenzie and screamed again. "You can't take my son from me. No! No! No!"

To my surprise, McKenzie did not slap me and I looked in his eyes and saw kindness there for the first time in the over 10 years we had been married.

"Julia, I'm not going to take him away from you. You need to rest now, Julia," he said.

"No, I don't believe you. No!"

He lowered his voice softly, not in menace but in sadness.

"Julia, dear, he's already gone. The lord has taken our boy. He's gone. Come, now. Rest. You must rest."

I realized then that in my delirium I had not seen that Jeremiah was dead. I saw that McKenzie mourned the loss of Jeremiah as much as I did and for the first time since we had boarded the train to Chicago, I took his hand willingly and allowed him to lead me to my bedroom.

McKenzie had brought my mother to assist in my convalescence and had been solicitous of anything that she had required of him. I believe that without her I would not have survived the loss of my son in addition to the infection that wracked my body as hard as it had Jeremiah's. I felt that with every pain I had that I deserved twice fold the pain because of my failure to prevent Jeremiah's death. I did not care whether McKenzie blamed me or not. I found it difficult to care for anything, even life.

And so it was my mother who kept me alive if by nothing else other than reminding me that I had to live in order to once more reunited with Jeremiah one day in heaven. I had to survive for him, she told me.

Now that three weeks have passed and I have survived the typhoid fever, I struggle to find the words to describe how our lives have changed.

They buried Jeremiah without me. The doctor insisted upon his immediate burial for community health reasons and I have yet to visit Jeremiah's grave, being kept abed although the worst of the fever has long since left me.

McKenzie has visited me daily and has treated me kindly, although I must admit I cannot be anything other than mildly agreeable with him. He has tried to comfort me and I have tried not to recoil at his attempts to as much as touch my hand or kiss my cheek. No matter how much kindness he offered, I could not forget the past.

I feared at first that he would blame me for Jeremiah's death, but I see now that he does not. This time there are no blinders of happiness to prevent me to seeing him as he is. I do not know how we will heal from this. I do not know how I will live without my little boy.

I simply do not know how I can wake up each morning without hearing his sweet voice and go to bed without his evening hugs.

Where is God now? I can only hope that he cares for my beautiful boy until I can be with him again.

Chapter Twenty-Six

Summer 2010

Juls put the journal down on the table and wiped the tears away from her face. She had never known of Jeremiah and this particular journal gave a completely different insight into both Julia and McKenzie. Somehow she had difficulty seeing him as the cold, sadistic rapist of whom Julia had previously written. For the first time, Julia had written more about McKenzie other than his sexual sadism and she had shown him to be a loving father and a man who was not singularly cruel and evil. He obviously had loved Julia in some way, although Juls was not sure how.

"I felt it important that you read this journal or I wouldn't have mentioned it," Jack said.

Julia nodded and turned her head to look out the window at the children playing in the summer sun down the street from her house. How could she not be moved by what she had just read? She felt more ambivalent than ever now. At least she had had a reason to hate McKenzie before she read this journal. Now, he was more of a real person to her rather than just a stereotype. As everything she had ever known about McKenzie had been from his descriptions within Julia's journals, she wondered if her own modern expectations of love, fidelity, and marriage had tinted her view of what she expected a 19th century husband to be.

She wiped the last of her tears away and shook her head. No, she thought. He might have changed with the birth of Jeremiah, but she still believed he was a cruel and greedy man who had taken Julia as his bride for her handsome dowry.

"I still find it difficult to see McKenzie as much more than a cruel man," she said to Jack.

Jack watched her face as she struggled to calm herself. The morning light flowing through the uncovered windows bathed her in a white light that lit her blonde hair and lightly tanned skin. The color of the sun from their Florida trip was beginning to fade from her skin, but the color there now was from the tears and the emotion of reading the journal.

"Juls, your dad told you it didn't matter. I can burn these things for you any time. Do you think that Julia would have wanted you to suffer?"

"Do you think that she kept the journals to punish McKenzie's descendant? I don't think so. I think she would be horrified to think that you felt guilty for something that you could not possibly have been responsible for," he said.

Juls nodded and lightly stroked her fingertips against the small journal. So much pain. So much heartbreak. Had Julia ever been happy after her marriage? Had she ever been happy?

Juls looked up to Jack. She couldn't let these be destroyed. They were all the evidence of who Julia was and what happened to her. Just the fact that no one in the family had ever know of her son, Jeremiah, was important enough for Juls to preserve them. Life was neither easy nor unbearably hard. It simply was. That was a lesson her great-great grandmother had taught her in just a short time.

"No, Jack. I want to keep them. I know you're lining up some other work, but I'm going to come back to them. I need to know the rest. Good or bad. I need to know. Even if I am the last of Julia's descendants, someone will bear witness to her life," Juls said.

Jack shrugged and picked up the journal and placed it back into its protective sleeve. He hadn't told Juls yet that he hadn't bothered to start looking for another story yet. He still had enough money from his last one to not worry for a while and for some reason he couldn't explain, he wasn't ready to leave Julia's story either. Every morning he got up, pulled out his laptop and cruised the web looking for leads, but eventually he ended up pulling one of the journals out of the trunk and reading.

While Juls left him every morning for work as he sat at the dining table with the laptop open with his Fiesta coffee mug, a yellow legal pad, and pen beside it, she had no idea of how he spent the rest of his day. Sometimes he spent the entire day reading the journals. Julia had been quite a writer and more than once he had wondered if Juls had inherited that gift from her grandmother, but Juls had never shown him anything she had ever written other than a shopping list or a note about a missed phone call.

Sometimes, when the journals were difficult to bear, he left them to walk down the short distance to Ritter Park where he made the small runner's loop, watching the runners, some of them tall, thin and running like gazelles down the hard packed path among the carefully manicured greens and trees.

On more than one occasion he had been reminded of Central Park when walking through Ritter Park. Though it was nowhere near as expansive and had no great buildings bordering it, it was a beautiful and large park for a small city. Beautiful turn of .the 20th century homes bordered it.

Other days he drove out to Barboursville to the Huntington Mall and wandered through the large mall, built in the same manner as most malls throughout the United States - a series of chain stores and boutiques anchored by the ubiquitous Sears, Penney's, and usually two large department stores.

In his early research of Huntington and Cabell County, he had discovered that Barboursville had been the site of the first county seat and courthouse. It was only after the county had been divided into much smaller counties, the growth of Guyandotte, and the eventual placement of Collis Huntington's city by the river that Barboursville had faded into a sleepy little village. Or, at least it had until the builders of the mall had chosen their town to be the best location for a mall when in-fighting among the city planners, property owners, and mall builders had eliminated the downtown area as a shopping venue for the mall.

But Jack had found Huntington a curious example of a city that reinvented itself as it needed and while the original downtown shops had mostly disappeared when the shoppers fled, the development of other businesses and stores had once more brought people back to Huntington.

And, there was always the 800 pound gorilla in the room – Marshall University, whose very presence swelled the city population each year by over 25,000 students with their many programs, from the medical school to the newly planned law school, not to mention the athletic programs which had produced athletes who had become NBA coaches and NFL players.

The school fed not only students into the city, but jobs and smaller businesses that clung to Marshall's fortunes much as remora that clung to the sides of a great white shark.

Huntington had gone from a collection of farms and a few ferry landings, to a railroad destination, to a steel and glass industrial city, to finally the town that supported a great university. It was a lot of change for 135 years or more for one city, Jack thought as he sometimes drove the streets looking for evidence of the town that Collis Huntington had begun. It did not surprise him that much of what had existed at the beginning was now gone, but then Julia's journals had explained how so many great floods from the Ohio River had played their own role in that particular drama.

Now Jack needed to decide what he was going to do with this life into which he had allowed himself to have fallen. He loved Juls. He knew that and he knew she loved him, though she rarely said the words. It was at night as she clung to him in her sleep as those Komodo Dragons were closing in on her and he stroked her hair and calmed her sleep that she would smile in her sleep and relax.

So this morning, which Juls had free and he ostensibly had, was a rare time when they sat down and talked about the journals. Jack had thought that Juls wanted nothing to do with the journals, but he saw that this one discovery had changed her mind. And, if that was to be what she wanted, then he would go along with her. He had no idea what their futures held, but he did know that they were no longer bound by the journals. Perhaps by one another, but not by the past.

Chapter Twenty-Seven

Diary of Julia Chafin Bell
1900

I have given birth to a new son this week. His name is Jonas and while I still mourn my poor lost Jeremiah these many years past, I am in awe of how a child conceived in true love can be so incredibly beautiful.

I have so many things for which to be thankful. First, McKenzie has no idea that Jonas is not his son. McKenzie struts about like a peacock, forgetting that he was unable to perform his husbandly duties in the months before Jonas's conception. He also does not notice that the child does not resemble him as our daughter Thea does. Jonas smiles angelically, his blonde hair curling around his face, making his small cheeks appear cherubic.

Thea was conceived shortly after Jeremiah left us. Surprisingly, McKenzie came to me as a husband normally would have after we lost Jeremiah. He never hurt me or punished me again, although he also never asked my consent, but then what good wife would deny her wifely duties? He has continued his habitation with his whores, but I have viewed that as a release, especially after the birth of Thea.

I know that McKenzie had hoped for the birth of another son when I informed him that I was with child again and he had not appeared too disappointed with her, though he seldom spent time with her as he had with Jeremiah. Poor Thea, she bore the sharp pointed features of her father. She would never be a great beauty, but her family's money would not make her unmarriageable.

She was so desperate for her father's approval that even at the age of eight she had developed the same haughty and self-indulgent personality as her father. I have tried to sway her from this attitude and from the path I saw she would approach as a young woman, but she is truly her father's daughter in every way except for his overweening confidence. And she masks that lack of confidence with airs of superiority. On more than one occasion I have had to scold her for her treatment of other children. I worry for her. I love her, but I see a poor future for her inability to love anyone.

My second thanksgiving is tinged with great guilt which I can only hope that the good Lord can forgive me. I had never intended to love a man after what McKenzie had done to me. There were times when I feared most men and I often wondered if all wives were tortured the way I had been. I sometimes would become angry at all the romantic books that are thrust upon young women, full of chivalric heroes on white chargers who swooped into the heroine's life to rescue her from dragons.

Even on my darkest nights, I could never have thought that a man was out there in the world who would rescue me from the loneliness and despair, from the heaviness of my heart, but he was there all along, unknown to me and waiting for me, waiting to make things right. He was McKenzie's attorney, Johnson Perry.

Johnson was much closer to my age and was unmarried for the first few years he had been McKenzie's attorney when he had married a young woman from Staunton, Virginia by the name of Susannah Lewis Hughes. Johnson had brought her to dine with us and I found her countenance quite pleasant and her presence very companionable, but at that time McKenzie had forbidden me to socialize with the wife of someone whom he considered an employee. This was at the beginning of our marriage and a most unbearable time and I so longed for the friendship of another woman.

Of course, this was also before we lost Jeremiah and McKenzie still treated most people not associated with the Huntington Railroad as his social inferiors with the exceptions of the Laidleys and the Buffingtons. It was as if our lost Jeremiah had humbled him in some way.

But by then it was too late for me to become friends with Susannah Perry. She had given birth shortly before the typhus epidemic to a son, Allen Lewis Perry. Her son was perfectly healthy, but Susannah became ill with typhus and died within days of my own loss.

Johnson was as bereft as I was, though I did not know it at the time. He had loved his wife, but he knew little about the raising of a child and had brought his sister-in-law Mary Hughes from Virginia to assist him in raising young Allen. Mary was ten years older than Johnson and a spinster who would be without a home when her parents died so she chose to come and reside with the Perrys rather than face a life of genteel poverty.

She had no feelings toward Johnson other than a shared grief for her dead sister, but she loved the child as if he had been her own and he thrived with her tutelage.

By this time McKenzie had loosened his hold upon me, and upon finding that Johnson's sister-in-law was a descendant of the Augusta County, Virginia Lewis family, allowed us to visit with one another. She became a close friend, something I had not had in my entirety as a married woman, but with her being an unmarried woman there were so many things which I was unable to discuss with her. How could anyone advise me on things which I was too shamed to broach with my own mother, much less a woman who had no knowledge of wifely duties?

Johnson often brought Mary and young Allen with him to visit when he knew he would be spending several hours with McKenzie and so not only did Mary and I become friends, but Johnson did as well. Our common grief bonded us although we never spoke of our losses. I believe that he felt the unbearable burden of what had been taken from him as I did. It was something I simply could not discuss. And I must give credit to McKenzie for this. He never discussed it either, although I sensed sometimes that he wanted to talk about Jeremiah and that he missed him as much as I did. I can only think that McKenzie in this one instance was kind enough not to discuss it because he knew how I hurt and for that I was thankful.

The problem with McKenzie after the typhus epidemic was that he increased his visits to Second Avenue and often forgot appointments with Johnson, who was left to be entertained by Mary and myself. I thought at first that we bored him with the silly prattling of women, but he never betrayed such emotions to us if he felt that way.

It was after the birth of Thea that Johnson and I found ourselves alone for the first time. Mary and young Allen were suffering from la grippe and dared not bring any contagion into a home where a new child was so Johnson came alone and as with past meetings with McKenzie was left sitting in wait.

That particular December day was brutally cold and I told Johnson that I doubted that McKenzie would return home that afternoon or evening. I was honest with him. It would have been hypocritical of me to pretend otherwise. He was quite aware of where my husband spent much time.

It was close to the Christmas festivities and my thoughts had been with Jeremiah constantly that day, wondering what he would have wanted from St. Nicholas or thinking of the joyous glow of the tree lighting reflected in his face. And so I found I could not hide my grief that night as I had in the past. I began to weep as I looked out at the ice upon the Ohio and Johnson tried to comfort me as best he could.

His tender touch helped me to find my way back to the present and by the time my weeping had quieted, I looked up into his pale blue eyes and waited for the kiss that I could feel we both wanted. I was lost within that kiss and I realized for the first time since my marriage to McKenzie that a man could love a woman with tenderness and strength simultaneously.

We found ourselves upon a wicker chaise in the solarium and loved one another with a desperate hunger that could not let go. Neither of us had planned it or spoken of it, but that night we fell in love.

As Johnson's presence was often seen at our house, no one questioned his continued visits after that night and our love grew stronger than any emotion I had ever felt. So, it was with great despair when I related to him that I was carrying his child. Had I been free, we could have had it all. But we both agreed that with the entanglements of an innocent child, we would have to end our assignations. McKenzie could never know. He would have killed or destroyed both of us and so we parted, both broken hearted and bereft again, with only the hope of our child to give us any joy.

And now Jonas is here with me and Johnson has distanced himself. He told me shortly after Jonas was born that he could hardly bear to see McKenzie claim Jonas as his child, but he would not disgrace me or have me shamed. He felt that he could maneuver McKenzie into working at his offices rather than at our home.

So I am alone again with just my two children for comfort. Surprisingly, Thea has shown a great tenderness and affection for her new brother. I hope for both their sakes that this affectionate bond will withstand time and the changes of life as they mature.

Chapter Twenty-Eight

Summer 2010

Jack sat stunned. How could he tell Juls this new discovery? The trials of Julia's life had been so difficult for her to absorb, but he knew that this revelation would be completely different. For the first time he also wondered if this might have explained more about Julia's murder, though he struggled to find a connection other than Jonas that would have made anyone within the family wish for her death. Perhaps Jonas could not bear the shame of being discovered as a child of adultery.

He placed the journal on the table and picked up his cell to call Juls and then stopped himself. This was not news he could deliver over the telephone. He wanted to be there for her in case the information caused her any further pain. He cursed himself for a fool for not having left Huntington and those damnable journals. He knew that Juls was losing her will to fight this anymore. She tossed more and more in her sleep each night, sometimes waking him with her screams.

If only he had taken that trunk of poison back to its place under the eaves and gone out into the world, he might have avoided having to watch her gradual fall into depression. No matter how hard he tried, he could not shake her from it and he had eventually spoken with both her parents about his concerns.

Her father wanted the journals destroyed immediately. Jack could sense a hatred for Juls's family roots in her father's tone, something he had never really heard before then. But Jack explained that he had tried to get rid of the books once and Juls had adamantly refused. He could only imagine how Juls's father would react to this latest information. At least her parents had been circumspect regarding Jack's conversations with them. He felt guilty going behind her back and discussing this with them, but he was also beginning to feel somewhat frantic about her state of mind.

What was the old saying, he thought? She looked like a beautiful swan serenely floating across the water, but paddling like mad below the surface just to stay afloat. Jack was afraid that too much more of this would be simply more than she could take.

The lawyer they had hired to research the matter of the money found in the journals and whether they would have to share it had found nothing yet to stop them from claiming the money as their own.

Jack was thinking of the conversations with the lawyer when he felt as if someone had slapped him hard across the face. The lawyer's name was Lewis Perry. How the hell had he missed that, Jack thought. And the coincidence. It was uncanny.

He was so lost in thought about this that he did not hear Juls come home or enter the dining room. He had been so engrossed in the journals and the lawyer situation that he had lost track of time.

"This is not the greeting I was hoping for," Juls said and sat down on his lap, kissing his forehead and smiling broadly.

God, he loved it when she smiled like that, Jack thought. He wished he could make her this happy all the time, but he knew that what he had to tell her this evening might wipe that gorgeous smile from her happy face.

He pulled her close to him and she laid her head upon his shoulder, wrapping her arms around him and relaxing against his broad chest.

"You must have had a great day," he said.

"Mm, yes, I did."

"I asked Schulte for more writing assignments and fewer editing tasks. He wasn't too happy at first, but when I told him that I missed writing enough to look for something else, he saw what I was really saying and gave me my first writing assignment in years."

She stood and headed toward the kitchen continuing to talk as she headed for the fridge in search of something to eat.

"I know it sounds silly to be so excited about writing something as simple as a press release, especially compared to what you do, but it felt good. I felt as if I were standing on my own for the first time," she said as she dug a bag of baby carrots from the fridge and bit into one.

Jack had followed her into the kitchen and he leaned against the kitchen counter and looked at the black and white tile floor. He did not want to do this. He closed his eyes for a moment and tried to wish the moment away with all his might.

Juls stopped eating the carrots and saw that Jack was upset, but she thought that he had found another story to follow and was trying to figure out how to tell her he was leaving.

Well, she thought, I've been preparing for this. I can smile and encourage him. I can do this. I can, she thought.

"Jack, what's wrong. Did you find your next book? That's great if you did. I know you're probably getting bored with this place," she said, unaware that her voice was quivering as she spoke and tried to smile.

He looked at her standing next to the old refrigerator, holding the bag of carrots, her face revealing all the emotions that she used to manage to keep hidden from him.

Damn it, he thought. Damn these fucking people. Juls did not deserve this.

He shook his head. "No, I haven't found anything yet. Well, that's not actually accurate. I haven't found a new topic yet is what I should say. But," he paused and took a deep breath, "I did find something very important in Julia's journals."

"What did you find?" she asked, her voice flat and emotionless. Whenever the topic of those journals came up, she shut herself down. The happy woman who had sat smiling upon his lap was gone in an instant, replaced by the Juls who answered the door the first time he came here.

"What did you find? Tell me. I can take it. I'm not going to fall apart, Jack. Tell me."

"I think you'd better let Julia's words tell you. I'm not sure where to even begin on this," he said.

She handed the carrots to him and briskly walked into the dining room where she found the journal he had been reading. She sat down and opened it.

"What date?" was her only question as she began to leaf through the pages. He told her and walked back to the kitchen and began to put some sort of meal together for them. He had no idea if she would want to eat after reading the journal entry, but he was getting hungry himself.

He had almost finished an omelet for her when she came back into the kitchen.

"Jesus Christ. Julia really had her secrets. So I'm not a Bell. Well, I guess I am, but not by blood. Well, that's good. I'm not McKenzie Bell's descendant. That's not bad news, Jack."

He flipped the omelet onto one of her Fiesta Ware plates and looked up to see her smiling again.

"You're not upset?"

"My god, no. I'm relieved. The man was . . . bad. He was a drunk and he slept with every woman he could. He tortured Julia for the first years of their marriage. God, no, I'm relieved. I'm relieved," she said and began to laugh a little too shrilly for his ears.

What he heard in her voice was not good. He moved to take her in his arms and she sidestepped him.

"What are you doing? I'm fine. I'm fine. You act like I'm going to fall apart. Jesus, Jack. Jesus. Just let me be," she said unaware that tears were streaming down her face.

Before she could move again, he folded her into his arms and held her tight, not letting her go although she fought the embrace. She continued pushing at him and he continued holding her tightly until she fell forward against his shirt and wept. She clung to him and held on to him as if she were slipping down into water, drowning under the weight of what she had read.

He lifted her up and carried her to his bed which had become their bed and laid her there, lying down next to her and letting her cry this out with no words spoken between them. As he felt her body shake against his, he wondered how much more of this she could take. At that moment he hated Julia, no matter what she had endured. She had no right to inflict any of this on Juls. Juls was an innocent and Julia was stripping that away with every entry.

He hated her. And he loved Juls. He knew that with no uncertainty now.

Chapter Twenty-Nine

March 25, 1937

Julia had completed her will and Allen Perry had taken great care to write it precisely the way she dictated it. She was leaving her children nothing. The property and any assets were to be sold upon her death with the local Salvation Army to receive any funds resulting from said sales.

What Allen Perry did not know was that there would be little left for her family to fight the Salvation Army over other than the house and its contents. She had been removing money from the bank for the past three years very slowly and placing the money safely in her house.

Allen's father Johnson had died several years ago and for the first time she felt nothing to tie her to this earth. She missed him far more than she ever thought she would. He had become her lawyer shortly after Johnson's death during the Spanish Flu epidemic. That had been a frightening time for her. She had been so afraid that Jonas or Thea would become ill and she refused to even allow herself to think that Johnson might fall ill.

But the flu had left everyone she loved untouched but him. When years earlier McKenzie had succumbed to alcoholism and dissipation, she could not weep for him. She did weep, but she wept for the 17 year old he had abused and almost destroyed. If people thought those tears were for him, so be it, she thought. But she did not shed one tear for the drunken man with whom she had been forced to spend a good part of her life.

Now she had to do the hardest thing of all. She had to tell Jonas the truth and she prayed he would forgive her. He was an intrinsic part of her plan to keep McKenzie's heirs from her money and without his help, she would be forced to rethink her entire scheme.

After the flood waters receded, she had returned to her home and had crews immediately begin working on cleaning the remains of the flood from her home. Her solarium was destroyed. It had actually been ripped from the brick house and all her orchids were gone. What had devastated her most was not the loss of the solarium, but the loss of a single piece of furniture - the wicker chaise longue upon which she had shared so many tender moments with Johnson.

It seemed as if God were punishing her for loving Johnson when she had been a married woman. She stood at the door to the solarium and instead of seeing the mud covered lawn and the debris strewn everywhere, she saw instead that wonderful night when she and Johnson had conceived their beautiful child.

The upper floors of her home were untouched and she was thankful she had placed her trunk of journals in a locked room on the third floor and her money in the safe in her bedroom. Everything still important was safe and her memories of Johnson could never be taken from her.

Once the cleaning had been completed and new, but rather sparse and somewhat cheap furnishings were placed on her first floor, she called Jonas to her home. For one of the few times in her life she had steeled herself for this conversation with a glass of bourbon and she had insisted that Jonas have a glass as well as she told him of the story of her life and his life as well.

"Nothing is easy, Jonas. No would have believed me and women are always forced to surrender to the will of their husbands. I was no different," she said.

The silence in the house was horrible. She had dismissed all her servants and she and Jonas were the only two people in the house.

Jonas did not speak. He appeared to be in a state of shock and she was concerned that he was about to leave her forever - unforgiven and despised. He looked so much like her lost Johnson, his thick shock of pale blond hair, his light blue eyes and refined features. If she were cursed and rejected by him her for her lies and infidelity, she did not think she could live with such pain. It would be as if she had lost Johnson once again.

Julia looked out the windows where the solarium used to be and sighed deeply.

"You have no idea how hard it is to love someone and never be allowed to be near them, to be with them," she said. "I loved your father almost as much as I loved you.

You must forgive us both. We loved each other and no one knew. No one was hurt. Even McKenzie never suspected and he was always keeping watch over my attachments, friends, and even my own brother's visits."

She did not tell him that after his birth that she and Johnson had never spent another intimate moment together, including after McKenzie's death. They shared their lives in a way that most people would never understand. She knew that there was nothing that Johnson would not do for her except for that.

"Of course, we could have married after McKenzie's death, but we never discussed it. It would have changed nothing and you could not know. We feared it might have done too much damage had we told you when you were younger," she said and paused long enough to drink some of the bourbon she had poured. The liquor burned her throat and made her a bit light-headed.

She started to stand and began to teeter as Jonas jumped up to steady her and assist her in sitting back down upon the cheap settee. She placed her hands upon the rough horsehair upholstery and stifled the fear she felt.

"I should have bought better furniture, but I did not want . . ." She left the sentence unfinished, the thought drifting upward away from the main concerns she was trying to confront.

"Mother, are you alright?" Jonas asked.

Julia looked up at him and tilted her head slightly as if seeing him differently than she had in the past. He did not appear to be angry with her. Instead, he was actually showing concern. Perhaps, she thought, he will forgive me for my deceptions.

"Yes," she said and took a deep breath. Nothing in the room smelled as it should. It was as if the flood had washed away any evidence of the life she had lived there. All she could smell was new lumber and cheap furniture.

"Jonas, I now must tell you that I am leaving everything, including this house to charity."

He started to speak, but she raised her hand and stopped him. He had to hear her out before he made his own decisions. She then explained her plan to him, the journals in the trunk and the money and jewels that he would remove from her home sometime soon, that he would tell no one about it, absolutely no one could know. She told him that he was her only heir and that if she left anything to him in her will that Thea and her children would suspect something and come after him.

She spent the next few hours explaining her problems with Thea and her sons, her fear of them and her inconsolable feelings of loss about his real father.

"It's too late, either way. I have made my will and Allen Perry has already taken the necessary precautions should anyone try to annul it."

"I should also tell you that Allen knows nothing of my relationship with your father. Allen is a good man and he is your true brother, but I implore you not to reveal any of this to him. I do not think Johnson would have wanted him to think less of him as his father," she added.

Throughout her long narration, Jonas had sipped his bourbon and nodded in agreement with her, sometimes questioning her about the details of the plan and even once making a plea to her for making some sort of provision for Thea.

"Absolutely not. I have given my last dime to that ungrateful child and McKenzie's descendants".

"She thinks me an idiot and weakling and thinks of my money as a fountain at which she may eternally drink. It is time she stood upon her own two feet and make her husband or wastrel sons help her. I will do no more," Julia said adamantly.

Jonas found her adamant about this. He did not want to see his sister impoverished. Thea had always been a handful, he had to admit even to himself, but she had always shown him great love. He pointed these things out to Julia.

"Jonas, she knows that as the eldest son that you will most likely be the heir to the Bell fortune. Do not trust her. I love her. She is my daughter. I cannot not help but love her. But, you must be wary of her and her sons. They will try to hurt you in order to take whatever they think I might give you. Promise me you will not take this advice lightly. Please, you must."

Jonas lowered his held and placed his hands upon his forehead. His entire life had changed in just a matter of hours. All of his plans had fallen through because his mother had fallen in love. Everything he had thought he knew was wrong.

"Mother, I will do whatever you want, but the money . . . I have my own that I have made. With the new development I have planned, I will financially be in good shape. Mack will join me in the project and one day carry on my business. I don't need to take this and leave Thea starving. I can't think about her hurting like that," he said.

Julia nodded her understanding, but said otherwise.

"Jonas, mark my words. Your sister will betray you and try to take everything you value in this life from you. Trust no one. Please."

Jonas stood and walked to the new windows overlooking the lawn and the river in the distance. He shook his head. He was not happy about this, but he would do what she asked. She had risked everything for him and he had to honor that if for no other reason.

He walked back to where she sat. She looked so small and frail for the first time in his life. He thought about what she had endured to survive the past 50 years and wondered how she had lived. All he wanted to do was make things right for her.

"I will do whatever you ask, Mother. I will protect you. I don't care about the money, but I do care about you and I will respect whatever you ask. I think you are wrong about Thea, but I will do as you ask."

He leaned over and kissed her cheek, the papery thin texture of her face so delicate beneath his hand. As he made his way to the foyer, he stopped in the doorway and turned to her as he placed his fedora upon his head.

"Mother, I love you. I'm . . . I'm sorry you've had to carry this burden. I'm not sure that I understand it, but it does not change how I feel. I will always love you," he said and left the house.

Chapter Thirty

Diary of Julia Chafin Bell
September 1937

Tonight Jonas will come for the trunk. The last of my plans will be complete and I will be able to rest now knowing that no blood of McKenzie will ever taint my family. I have waited 50 years and now I will see my final revenge upon that monster. Nothing he ever touched thrived and nothing ever will now.

I only wish I could laugh in his face and tell him the truth about everything. I know that I should let this hatred go, but I cannot. He thought to destroy me and I have done that to him. I have waited so long for this, but knowing that my true love's child will prosper and live on is the most I can ask for in this life.

I have spent the last week placing the money in the journals and the jewelry beneath the false bottom of the trunk. Everything but my wedding ring and earrings will be safely in Jonas's hands. His future and that of his children will forever be secure.

Tonight, I am waiting for him. Tonight, I am waiting for a lifetime of pain to finally cease. Victory shall be mine and McKenzie may burn in hell. Tonight. Tonight.

Chapter Thirty-One

Summer 2010

Juls had insisted on going into the office the next morning although she looked as if she had not slept in weeks. She refused breakfast and only drank the coffee Jack had made while she showered and dressed for work.

Jack's concern was growing with each hour.

"Tell me what to do, Juls," Jack had pled as they stood in the small kitchen across from one another drinking their coffee.

"I'll do whatever you want, but you can't go on like this any more. This has to end, one way or another," he said.

She just shook her head and sat her mug upon the counter and gathered her bag and keys together.

"I can't think about this now, Jack. I have too much work to do. We can talk about it later," she said.

Jack slammed his mug down on the table.

"Damn it, Juls. This is not my family. This is not my decision. Stop putting this off. This has gone on long enough," he said.

Juls hurried from the kitchen and down the hallway towards the front hall.

"Juls, stop it. Stop!"

She did as he commanded, but did not turn to look at him. The mask had come down again and she was shutting him out again.

"Juls, you know I love you. I would do anything to take this pain away from you. I want a life with you, not just a day to day thing where I don't even know if you're going to be there the next minute, much less the next day."

Jack walked around her and placed his hands on her forearms. He could feel her trembling and he was so afraid to let her walk out that door right now. He was terrified if she walked out he would never see her again.

"Juls, please, look up at me. Help me. Tell me what you want," he said.

She looked up at him, her pale blue eyes brimming with tears.

"I want you. Isn't that enough?" she asked and pulled away from him and walked out the door to her car to head downtown to her office.

Jack watched her drive away and leaned against the door frame, his hands dug deep into his pockets. For the first time in his life he prayed that she would come home safely that night. He felt a cool wind blowing from the northeast and felt the first crisp signs of autumn in the air. It was September now, almost three months to the day since he had first knocked on her door. And he felt stuck in reverse as if the last three months had been nothing but a painful lesson in futility. He wasn't sure if Juls would change or if he could help her. He wasn't sure if she wanted his help, but he couldn't leave her like this. He had to try to fix things somehow.

He closed the door and headed into the dining room and started digging through the journals until he found the ones from the 1930s. Surely there was something there in those last months that would give him a clue as to what had happened to Julia.

First he read the 1936 entries and found little there except daily activities and minutiae that didn't help at all.

It was when he came to the 1937 journals that he finally found what he had been looking for – why Julia had put the money in the journals, where they had gone and how she had feared Thea and her sons.

When he came to the final entry in the next to last journal, he was stunned and knelt in front of the trunk, removing the journals left in there and stacking them haphazardly to the side of his body and the trunk.

When he finally removed the last of them he felt for a loose board or anything that might open the false bottom of the trunk which Julia had written about in that last entry.

The fabric shredded a little as he tried to find a way to remove the bottom. He grimaced at that. He didn't want Juls to come home and find the trunk destroyed. This trunk meant too much to her.

Just as he was about to give up hope he found a think ribbon wedged between the board and the side of trunk. He pulled at the ribbon and the entire bottom of the trunk lifted upwards. As he looked down upon what he saw there he sat back and dropped the board.

Oh my god, Juls. Oh my god; he thought.

What had Julia done?

He leaned forward again and looked back into the trunk. Amidst the leather boxes lining the bottom and loosely wrapped jewels lay a single journal. The 1937 journal must not have been Julia's last one. But why put it here under this false bottom?

Jack took the journal out and leafed through it. There was no money in it and he realized that the handwriting was not Julia's. What the hell, he thought and turned to the first page and began to read.

When he heard the front door open a few hours later, he put the journal back beneath the false bottom and ran to meet Juls at the front door. She had left work early. He felt such relief. She had come back to him.

As he approached her in the hallway, he saw that she had been crying again. Oh, Juls. Juls. Don't. He started to open his mouth to tell her what he had found and she spoke before he could.

"I quit my job, Jack. I was trying to write a press release and couldn't even think of the first thing to write. I sat there for three hours and my mind was completely blank. I think something's terribly wrong with me."

He embraced her and held her closely as she hugged him to her thin body. He hadn't seen how much weight she had lost in the last few months, but he saw now that her clothes hung on her frame and her face was gaunt. All the color from their trip to Florida was completely gone.

He lifted her face with his hands and held it as he kissed her and smiled.

"It's going to be ok, Juls. I've found everything. You won't believe what I've found. It's all going to be ok. Trust me. But first, I need you to come in the kitchen and eat something. Come on and then I'll show you everything."

Juls walked with him back to the kitchen her arm wrapped around his waist as much for comfort as for support. After he had made an omelet for them, he led her into the dining room where the remaining journals were spread across the floor.

"What have you done, Jack?"

He smiled and lifted the false bottom.

"I found the truth, Juls. I found the truth. Jonas, your great-grandfather, was truly innocent and I've found his own testament to what really happened."

Juls was amazed by what she saw under the thin wood bottom. Every piece of jewelry her grandmother had ever owned was there except for the pieces supposedly taken when she had been murdered. Each of the boxes held parures and demi-parures of diamonds, rubies, pearls, and emeralds, all set in 24 karat gold. Some of the necklaces of lesser value were wrapped in thin silk squares of fabric and she could see the faint shimmer of strands of pearls and the muted glitter of topaz and gold necklaces.

She opened one of the leather boxes, the leather thick and rough like the skin of a lizard. Inside was a diamond and cobalt blue sapphire parure, the white diamonds shining next to the glittering blue with a very large carat diamond pendant suspended from the center of the choker style necklace. She removed the necklace and held it to her throat. The metal and stones felt cold against her skin.

Jack watched her in fascination. It was the first real smile he had seen on her face in weeks. He laughed out loud and she began to laugh with him.

"I guess I don't have to worry about quitting my job," she said and they began to laugh even harder.

"This is incredible, Jack. Is it worth much? Will it change the estate?" she asked.

Jack shook his head and handed her the last two journals.

"Read these. There is no claim against the estate. You and your father are the last descendants of Jonas and this belonged to him. All of it. Even if Julia had other descendants, she gave this to Jonas weeks before she died. No one else had a claim on it. It went from him to your grandfather Mack to your father and you," he said.

"Read them. Now. Now." He stood and went back to the kitchen leaving her sitting in the floor with the last two journals. The last one from Julia explained everything about where the money had gone and how.

Juls smiled as she read about Julia's final revenge against McKenzie. She felt proud of her grandmother's tenacity. But, the biggest surprises came when she began to read the last journal. It was at that point that she felt her life begin to turn itself right side up.

Chapter Thirty-Two

Journal of Jonas Christopher Bell
September 1937

Mother is gone. I cannot believe it. I walked to the river and sat down upon the bank and wept as I have not since I was a small boy.

After a while I just sat there and watched the barges pass by and wondered how many times in her life she had done the same thing. She must have been so lonely, but in the last few weeks she had finally seemed happy, that is until Thea had gone to visit her.

I could hear Thea's shrill voice all the way over here at our house and I looked to Louise and Mack as if to question whether I should go over there. But before I could decide, I saw through our dining window Thea's car speeding off and I knew then that somehow Thea had figured out that Mother was disinheriting all of us. I also knew then that I would have to feign surprise over it with even Louise and Mack, but I didn't mind. They would never question it. And one day, Mack would know the truth.

But now everything was wrong. Mother was dead. Old Effie had shown up that morning and found the front door of the house standing open. She had walked in calling Mother's name, but the house was silent. It was only when she walked into the main foyer that she discovered Mother's body in the floor in a pool of blood, a hatpin piercing the back of Mother's neck, the floral hat she had been wearing hanging against her back, dark and blood soaked.

Effie's screams had brought everyone, including myself and Mack running to Mother's home. We saw Mother lying there and I longed to pick her up and do something, anything. My first impulse was to gather her up in my arms and carry her to the sofa so she might rest more comfortably, but common sense stopped me, no matter how painful seeing her lying there was. I instead went to the old Western Electric wall phone that had hung in the kitchen for decades and dialed the operator to ask them to send the police to Mother's home immediately.

Mack, Effie, Louise, and I were questioned by the police for hours. They told us that Mother's safe had been emptied, although I knew that there was very little money there, and then they reported that her jewelry was missing, which I also knew was not taken by a thief and would not be found.

Thea and her useless sons arrived later and she began to wail so loudly that the ambulance crew was about to take her to the hospital when she suddenly composed herself, almost a little too quickly for my tastes. I remembered Mother's words to me not to trust her and I knew I should have listened, but I was grieving as much as I thought she was and I wanted to give her comfort.

When I approached her to help her, she stood and pointed her finger at me and screamed, "Murderer! You did this! You knew she was planning to disinherit us all and you killed her!"

I was so taken aback by her accusations that I could not believe what I was hearing. Had my own sister just accused me of murder? How could she do this? It was simply not possible.

Mack stepped forward and tried to calm Thea down.

"Now, Aunt Thea, you know Father would never harm Grandmother. You're just distraught. Please, don't say such things," he said.

Thea violently shook his arm from her and looked to the policemen standing there,

"He probably helped his father. I wouldn't be surprised if they had planned it all. I tell you if you search their house you'll find mother's things," she said.

"Enough, Thea!" I said.

"How can you say such things to me and to your family? You know what you're saying is preposterous."

I was shaking as I responded to her accusations, as much from shock as from fear that the police might actually believe such nonsense. But I was even more shocked when I found that the police were actually listening to her accusations with a serious ear.

I grabbed Mack by the arm and led him from the house, telling all of them that if they needed me further that they could find me at my home, making arrangements for my mother to be taken care of.

But, the first thing I did when Mack and I entered our home and before they would come to question us, I called Allen Perry, told him what had happened, and asked him if he could come to my home as soon as possible. Then I walked down to the river and sat and waited. I was still sitting there when the police appeared behind me and asked me to return into my home to speak with them.

God help me, but Mother was right and I saw then that I would be mourning not only her loss, but the rest of my family as well.

Chapter Thirty-Three

Journal of Jonas Christopher Bell
October 1937

Where do I begin to even try to write of the events that have transpired in the last few weeks? I have been arrested and indicted for Mother's murder. It is almost more than I can bear. There is no evidence except for Thea's accusation and the will.

I could have cleared my name at any time by simply producing the journals which I had hidden in the first home we had built in Bell Park, but I knew to do so would destroy my Mother's fine reputation and that I would not do.

So I suffered through endless miserable hours, being both browbeaten and at times physically abused by policemen trying to force a confession from me which I refused to utter. This made them even more frustrated in their attempts and they wrenched my arm so badly at one point that I thought it was broken.

I did have solace in the knowledge that the police had not included Mack in their pursuit of Thea's pointed finger. She should have pointed that finger at her own sons, I thought.

Mack,, thank the lord, was safe. Allen Perry represented me as much as possible and it was rather strange sitting across from him, knowing that he was my brother and being unable to tell him. But I honored Mother's wishes in every way. I just do not believe that she would have wanted any of this, but I made a promise to her and I cannot go back now.

I sit in jail having been refused bail by Judge Hayden with whom I am unfamiliar. I was never the political creature that my . . . that the man I had called my father was. I was happy to build things, to create a life for my family and make an area for other families to make their home in a pleasant atmosphere.

Mack came to visit me daily, bringing me food and short notes from his mother to me. I told him not to allow his mother to visit me. I did not want the taint of this horrible scandal to touch Louisa. I felt that seeing me in this terrible place might cause her untold grief.

So she tried to comfort me with my favorite foods and sweet love notes of her faith and trust in my innocence. I decided that I would not tell Mack about his grandmother's trunk and its contents until after this nightmare had concluded. Either way, I knew that the contents of it could not be touched for years without the police placing Mack as a suspect as well as myself if it were found.

Luckily, they never considered searching the few homes already completed in Bell Park and so the trunk which I had hidden far beneath the eaves of the best of the small cottages was not found by them. This spared my mother humiliation and safely secured Mack's future as well as sparing any of us from further speculations of guilt. But most importantly it protected my mother's reputation had the journals become public knowledge.

Better to swallow my pride and surrender my freedom and possibly my future and good name than have hers destroyed.

Had Thea discovered that I and my son were not McKenzie Bell's descendants or that Allen Perry was the son of mother's lover, she would have used that disgrace to prop up her own sick ideals of social standing.

Mother had been so right about Thea; but, god help me, I do understand that fear drives her frustration and envy. She is my sister and I love her in spite of the horror she has brought into my life.

I have spent many hours wondering about what had happened to Mother. Had she been robbed and murdered? Had someone found her dead and ransacked the place afterward? How had the hatpin pierced her neck? It was such an unlikely weapon. I could imagine a fiercer weapon being used than a thin hatpin. It simply made no sense to me.

The coroner's inquest is tomorrow and possibly there will be more information on her death. I must admit that I have entertained the thought that one of Thea's sons might have hurt Mother. After all, I did not see who was driving Thea's car from Mother's that afternoon. Could one or both of the boys have done this? I shudder to think that her grandchildren might be capable of such an act.

Either way, tomorrow will be a day where my life will be changed, perhaps forever. I can only pray that my family is protected.

Chapter Thirty-Four

Journal of Jonas Christopher Bell
October 1937

I cannot believe that I am at home with my family tonight. It seems as if god had sent kinder angels to protect them from the further disgrace of my standing trial and being imprisoned and even possibly executed for my mother's death.

The courtroom where the coroner's inquest occurred was packed with reporters and men I knew from the city and curiosity seekers in search of shocking and morbid details relating to my mother's death. Mack and Allen sat with me. Once more I had asked Louisa to remain at home. This was not a circus in which I wished her to be in attendance. Protecting her from the gossipmongers and the cameras and reporters was first and foremost in my heart. No matter what would happen to me, she would be safe.

Across the courtroom, behind the prosecutor's table sat my sister and her two sons. She somehow managed to appear both grieving and preening simultaneously. I was once more shocked by just how correct my mother's predictions about her actions had been. Her sons were worse. The eldest, Reggie, leaned back in a chair and smiled and waved at various members of the audience, even openly flirting with several pretty young women in the row behind him as if the whole event were something for his own promotion and entertainment.

Thea's younger son, Kent, was curiously quiet and subdued. I realized at that point that he had said very little during the past few weeks and had shunned all newspaper accounts where his brother and his mother had seemed to seek them out. He looked to me and to Mack only once or twice and both time his eyes were filled with anger and hatred. I suddenly recognized those angry eyes from my "father" McKenzie and I was afraid that he might have been the instrument of my mother's demise.

Mother had always been right and I became deeply worried that Kent might come after my family next if he thought we had robbed him of his inheritance.

And so Judge Hayden entered the room and we stood as the bailiff called for the coroner to come forward to deliver the results of his inquest. Both the prosecutor and Allen would be allowed to question the results, but in the end everyone knew that the Judge would most likely defer to the coroner's decision.

It was painful to hear him speak of mother as some woman without a name or family or people who loved and respected her. His physical description of her body was particularly difficult for me to hear and I looked to Mack and saw him grimace and hold his hand to shield his eyes on more than one occasion during the coroner's rather clinical description of Mother. At the same time, I noticed that Reggie was ignoring most of the testimony, still flirting silently with the girls behind him, and that Thea sat with a cold and emotionless look upon her face that bespoke of smugness. The entire time she held her purse on her lap and stroked it like some pet cat. Kent listened intently to every detail and his eyes continued to burn with the hatred I had witnessed earlier. I was beginning to believe more and more that he had been the agent of Mother's demise.

And it was then that the most shocking blow was delivered to us all by the coroner. After his long and clinical speech, he concluded with a final verdict – my mother had died not from murder, but from heart failure.

The people in the courtroom began rumbling about incompetence and asking what had happened to the money. The prosecutor stood and objected to the conclusion and said that it was well know that Julia Bell had been murdered by the insertion of a hatpin into her carotid artery. Allen looked to me in puzzlement, but remained quiet for the moment.

Judge Hayden turned to the coroner and asked how such a verdict were possible considering the way in which Mrs. Bell's body had been found. The coroner was a soft spoken man who had spent most of his life as a doctor in the community. He described the fact that mother had most likely suffered a severe coronary event and that she had fallen at that point, probably impaling herself with the hatpin through the throat. He said that she was probably unaware of any events following the coronary event and that the minimal amount of blood found at the scene supported his theory in that her heart had stopped pumping blood before the hatpin had pierced her neck. He said that had the hatpin been inserted in the artery prior to her heart stopping that there would have been found copious amounts of blood instead of the small pool beneath her head.

The judge asked him if he was ruling the death to be accidental or the result of foul play. The coroner hedged for a moment and said that while foul play could have led to the heart attack and that he could not state that it had not definitively, that it was most unlikely and that his verdict was that Julia Bell had died from natural causes precipitated by a cardiac event.

Once again the prosecutor objected and this time Allen stood as well, interrupting the prosecutor's harangue of the coroner. He requested that as the coroner had ruled the death to be of natural causes that I should be released immediately as no murder had occurred.

The judge pounded the gavel to quiet the courtroom and looked around it as if to judge his own performance in public opinion there rather than my own innocence. He knew, however, that even should he allow the prosecutor to continue with his case that an appeal would most likely overrule any decision he might make in opposition to the coroner's verdict.

He announced that all charges pending against me were to be dropped without prejudice and that I was to be released immediately. Allen grimaced slightly and I touched his elbow and whispered into his ear and asked if there was a problem. He nodded his head and whispered back to me that the phrase "without prejudice" meant that the prosecutor could open the case against me or even a member of my family at any time.

Then Allen did something completely unexpected. He embraced me and again whispered into my ear. "I would have fought for you, Jonas. I would never let my brother be prosecuted when he was innocent."

I pulled back from him and stared at him in shock. He smiled at me and walked away before I could say another word and although I wanted to follow him, my son had turned me around and was hugging me and grinning broadly, exclaiming loudly that he knew that justice would be served there today.

But no one else approached me to congratulate me or even speak to me. The men I had grown up with, the men who shared their own secret peccadilloes with me knowing my discretion, the men I had called friends – none of them looked my way or nodded their agreement with the verdict.

Thea and her sons left without speaking to me as well, although as Mack and I were leaving the courthouse, we noticed that she was holding court on the front lawn of the courthouse with a gaggle of newsmen. I still find it difficult to believe that she could betray me so much.

Louisa greeted me by running from the house to my arms, weeping as if she had not seen me in months rather than weeks. I spent several hours calming her and reassuring her that the entire matter was now ended. I failed to disclose to her that the police could arrest me again or even Mack, for that matter. I don't believe that Mack clearly understood the nature of the delivery of the verdict himself.

So, after a fine meal and the loving graces of my wife and son, I wandered from the house once more out toward the bank of the Ohio behind our home, this time taking a moment to turn and look back at what I had almost lost and then turning my head to face my mother's empty home.

Because of Thea's selfish behavior I had been denied any final good-byes to Mother. After the police had arrested me, they had held me without bail and had made it impossible to see to Mother's final arrangements. Instead, Thea had taken the reins of that particular endeavor and had flatly told both Louisa and Mack that their presence was not required nor invited to the proceedings. Mother had been buried in the south hills in some new cemetery with only three members of her family in attendance except for Thea's devoted coterie of fawning women.

I shook my head at the entire thought of Mother being buried alone by strangers and the people who may have well been responsible in some way for her death and it angered me so much. I would have stood on the riverbank brooding until darkness fell had not my sweet Louisa called from the back porch of the house for me to come in.

I was very worried about more than just what had happened to my mother. Looking at Louisa standing on the porch waiting for me, I began to worry about her and Mack as well. I feared that the reactions of the businessmen I knew and people with whom we often socialized in the past did not bode well for future business dealings. And for the first time I now worry about my family's future. I cannot risk using any of the money Mother had given me, especially if could endanger Mack's life. Many years would have to pass before I could reveal that secret to Mack and I suddenly saw that if Bell Park failed, my family would fail and become impoverished.

As I write this, I realize that nothing will ever be the same for my family again. The only positive thing to come of it was my knowledge that Allen accepted me as his brother and I hoped that at least in that there would be more than wishful thinking.

This is the last entry I am going to write about this entire debacle. I will place this journal with Mother's in the trunk in the house at Bell Park and I will give Mack the keys to that house. He will own it without any encumbrances, even if Bell Park is not further developed. He, at least, will have a secure home that is not tied to my fortunes.

Chapter Thirty-Five

Summer 2010

Juls quietly wept as she read her great-grandfather's words. He had paid such a great price for his son and her father and for her. If he had not protected them and protected Julia's secret, he would have been forgiven easily and the taint of the murder accusations would never have followed his memory or his descendants.

He had been placed in an impossible situation and had taken what fate had given him without question or complaint. His journal had made it clear that no one knew what had happened to Julia that last night.

Juls looked up from the floor where she had not moved as she had read the journals to find Jack standing above her, with a cup of coffee in offering to her. She smiled at him and felt her knees ache as she stood after having sat on the wooden floor for so long without moving.

She sat at the dining table where Jack joined her and drank in the hot strong coffee. Jonas had sacrificed so much for his descendants. It just was not fair.

"He gave up everything. He could have had it all," she said and sighed.

Jack took her hand and leaned forward.

"I don't think he ever intended for your grandfather or father to have lived in the dire straits that they found themselves in. Do you know what happened to him?" he asked.

Juls shook her head.

"We never, never discussed him or the "murder". I know that at some point the house on the river was sold and that Mack moved in here. I think his mother may have moved in here as well, but I'm not sure. I actually know more about Mack's later life than his earlier life. He served in World War II and was at Normandy on D-Day. I always thought that it was incredible that he survived that," she said.

"Oh god, Jack, now that I think of it, even Jonas's own family blamed him. Why else did they never speak of him or the murder? And why, in all the things that have been written about Julia's supposed murder, has no one ever bothered to discuss the coroner's inquest and the verdict of death by natural causes?" Juls continued.

This time Jack shook his head and shrugged.

"Probably because it didn't make interesting reading. A good juicy scandal just appeals to a more prurient and a much larger reading audience. It's human nature, I suppose. The way people slow down to look at car wrecks. What I found truly strange was that the records of the coroner's findings and the actual inquest are missing from the courthouse. Someone went to a great deal of trouble to make it seem as if Jonas had indeed been a killer."

"You know that Bell Park was a failure before the war. Only a few houses were built. I guess that's when everything else was sold off. Thank god Mack never sold this place," Juls said.

Juls looked over at the stacks of journals and the trunk with a hidden cache full of precious jewelry.

"Jonas died in 1938," Jack said. "Did you know that he was killed by a drunken teamster taking a load of whiskey downtown when he was crossing the street to go to the small bank across Third Avenue? According to everything I've read, he was killed instantly. I have a theory that he never had a chance to tell Mack about the trunk. You know, if Mack had sold this house, you would have nothing and you would probably have never discovered the truth about Julia's death."

Juls sat her cup down on the table and leaned toward Jack and stroked his face gently. She removed his glasses and kissed him. He was so handsome without his Clark Kent disguise. She marveled at how a man could have such beautiful eyes and such long eyelashes. She kissed him again, nibbling lightly at his lower lip and then smiled brightly at him.

"If you keep that up, you're going to find yourself with a whole different set of problems," Jack said and laughed.

"Jack, I can make this right, can't I?" she stated more than asked.

He leaned back and saw that she was beginning to see what he had seen when he had discovered Jonas's journal. He nodded his head and sipped his coffee.

"I can prove his innocence with these journals. Times have changed and anyone who knew either Julia or Jonas is long since gone. No one would blame her for her love of Johnson or her righteous hatred of McKenzie Bell. I can do this. I can give him back his name," she said.

Jack nodded and then took her hand in his again.

"I think you need to talk to your dad again, though. Jonas was his grandfather. I don't think he'll feel differently than you do, but you should talk to him first," he said.

"You're right. Oh, Jack. All this jewelry and the money. Can Thea's descendants claim any of it? Is it really ours?"

"Yours. And, no, I don't think so, but then I'm not a lawyer. It's funny that you have Allen Perry's grandson as your lawyer. It's as if your family knew they could trust them intuitively," he said.

He stood up and walked over to the trunk and closed the lid on it. Part of him wanted to take the jewelry out of it and take Juls into the bedroom and dress her in nothing but the diamonds. He smiled at that thought and walked back to her and took her hand.

"Will you help me write it?" she asked?

"Nope," he said. "It's all yours and rightfully so. I'll help you with editing and proofreading, but not writing. That's yours to do and your name should appear there."

"You mean you'll stay with me? Here?" she asked.

"Juls, I'll stay with you where ever you want to be. Here or in another city or even another country. Besides, I think I might like being a kept man," he said and laughed.

She draped her arms around his neck and pulled him close to her, the thin silk of her blouse a flimsy barrier between them.

"Well, then you'd better start making me happy right now because I am now a very rich woman and I want you," she said laughing with him.

He picked her up and headed towards the back bedroom where they had been sleeping.

"We have tonight and so many more and no more dragons," he said and closed the bedroom door behind them.

"Oh god, yes, the dragons are finally gone," she said and laughed as they lay down upon the bed.

ABOUT THE AUTHOR

Reneé Porter is the author of the series of novels,
The Taliaferro Chronicles, including *The 13th Victim*. The
next volume in The Taliaferro Chronicles, *Broken Rainbow*,
will be published in Autumn 2011.